MW00719646

Printed in the United States of America

Published by Pisgah Press, LLC
PO Box 9663, Asheville, NC 28815
www.pisgahpress.com

Book & cover design: A. D. Reed, MyOwnEditor.com

Library of Congress Cataloging-in-Publication Data
Wilson, Robert F.
The Pot Professor/Wilson

Includes bibliographical references and index

ISBN-13: 9781942016502

First Edition
First Printing
October 2019

The Pot Professor

RF Wilson

Acknowledgments

Peter Stanz, good friend and first reader of the manuscript of *The Pot Professor*.

The Mysterians mystery critique group, without whose regular feedback this novel would not have come to fruition.

My family for their continuing support and encouragement.

And **Beth Gage**, my great love, for everything she does to make it possible for me to spend great gobs of time at the computer.

Contents

"It's easy, after all, not to be a writer. Most people aren't writers, and very little harm comes to them."

JULIAN BARNES, Flaubert's Parrot

The Pot Professor

One

Tuesday

A cup of coffee and the morning paper stared up at me from the dining room table. Rain drummed on the deck beyond the double glass doors. The dog dozed at my feet; the cats held down opposite ends of the living room couch. When the kitchen phone rang, I considered letting it go to voice mail before acknowledging that a call at 6:30 in the morning could be important.

"Peters and—"

The caller cut me off.

"They're screwin' with me again, Ryder." I knew the voice.

"And the top o' the mornin' to you, Queenie. And, who might 'they' be?"

"Read the paper yet?"

"Actually, I was just getting ready to when I was interrupted by a phone call."

"Yeah, sorry to bother you. Look on page three."

I walked back to the table. The headline jumped out, as headlines are designed to do.

"Pot Professor" Found Dead On Weaver's Mountain

"That's an attention-getter."

"Read the article," she directed. "I'll hang on."

I complied.

> Yesterday afternoon the body of a man identified as Marcellus Revis, a resident of Colorado, was found dead in an outbuilding in the northwest area of the county. Dr. Revis had come to the area to participate in a conference on the medical uses of marijuana and was staying in a guest house on the property of Ms. Queenie Weaver ...

I set the paper down and picked up the phone again.

"I take it that when you say, 'they're screwing' with you, you're referring to your friends in the law and order business. The sheriff's people, perhaps?"

"None other than."

Queenie Weaver's run-ins with local law enforcement and criminal justice establishments were legion. During the civil rights agitation of the 1960s she'd been jailed multiple times for disturbing the peace, obstructing traffic, resisting arrest, and whatever other infractions could be hung on her. The authorities suspected she grew marijuana up on her mountain, though the "evil weed" was never detected on her person or her property ... until a young man was found dead at the bottom of a waterfall on her property a few years back. During that investigation investigation, a small plot of Maryjane was found at the edge of her land. She was ultimately cleared of all charges relating to the boy's death and the illegal drug, but her reputation with the law enforcement establishment was further enshrined.

"I imagine they're wallowing in schadenfreude over there," I said.

"Save the big words for your lawyer friends."

"It means they get to gloat."

"I been to college, too, Ryder. I know what it means. And, yeah, they're doin' that all right. They were out here searchin' the shed and the cabin. Wanted to search my house and the big barn, for heaven's sake. What the hell's my house or barn got to do with a body in the shed? I tried to get a hold of Nate, but, well, you know Nate."

I did know Nate. Nate Chatham. Civil rights champion. Defender of the oppressed and downtrodden, now semi-retired, for whom Kathy and I did an occasional investigation as when we worked with him to exonerate Queenie from her last imbroglio with the law. The man was notoriously unavailable.

"You want me to come out?" I asked.

"Nah. But I thought you ought to know what's happening. You might wind up working on my behalf again."

"We had so much fun the last time, why not do it again, you mean?"

"As much fun as it was—and I admit it was fun bein' able to stick my thumb in the eyes of those people downtown— I'd rather skip the opportunity for a replay, if it's all the same. Right now I think I need to go down to the four-lane and see if someone's put up a sign says, Welcome to Weaver's Mountain—a good place to get killed."

I took Kathy her morning cup of tea which she would sip in bed watching the news, one of the few times in our house when the idiot box claimed our attention.

"I heard the phone ring," she said. "New client?"

"Returning client, possibly."

She looked expectantly, like a dog does when you hold a treat in front of its face.

"Do tell."

"Queenie."

"Queenie? What's she up to now?"

"Allowing people to die on her property."

"Gee. You'd think she'd had enough of that."

"I do think it's getting kind of old."

I handed her the newspaper. After reading the article, she said, "Maybe there's some weird magnetism up there that attracts this stuff. Why was she calling you?"

"She couldn't get a hold of Nate—"

"Now there's a surprise."

"Right. So, she called me thinking we'll probably wind up getting involved in this."

"Does she think she's going to be arrested again?"

"She didn't say, but the sheriff's people have been out there already to search the place. If you remember the last time someone died on her property, there was no physical evidence to tie her to the death of that young man, yet they arrested her anyway."

"There was the marijuana complication," Kathy added.

"True. But that didn't warrant a murder charge. And the pot growing thing wound up getting thrown out, too."

"I think we ought to go out to see her."

"She already declined my offer to visit."

"I know she doesn't want to appear to need other peoples' help but I believe she'd appreciate the support. She's been through a lot up there in the last few years."

We were on our way out of the house when the landline rang again. This time Kathy picked up. When I heard her deep sigh, I knew it was her father on the other end.

"Hi, Dad ... Yes ... If I hadn't heard from you by tomorrow I would have given you a call. I am not ignoring you ... Have you been taking your medication? Getting exercise?... Then don't gripe, Dad. Do what you're supposed to do, and you'll probably feel better ... Please don't go there, Dad. I'll be up as soon as I can find the time. We are in business for ourselves, you know. If Rick and I don't do the work, the work won't get done and we won't get paid. It's as simple as that ... I can't speak for my brother ... Yes, you're lucky to have a daughter-in-law like Bethany ... Rick and I were just out the door to see a client when you called, Dad. I'll call you back in a day or two ... Yes ... I'll say, 'Hi' to him ... I love you, too."

After she hung up, she looked at me and said, "You know I'm going to have to go up there soon or it's just going to get worse. But he is so unpleasant to be around. No wonder my brother stays away, too."

"I'm sure I could cover things whenever you wanted to get away," I said.

"The problem is I don't want to get away. But I think I should."

"I'll do whatever I can to make it easier for you."

"You can be the daughter for a while."

"Not sure how that would work."

"Me neither. Let's go see Queenie. I always feel better after being out on Weaver Mountain in spite of its history of untimely deaths."

I have only one arm, the result of a drunk driving accident when I was eighteen in which a young girl was killed. It took me the better part of twenty years to come to terms with both the destruction I caused in the lives of others and my own disfigurement and "limited ability" status. Kathy helped keep me on an even keel. Whenever I showed signs of "poor-me-ism," she helpfully pointed out that one arm is better than no arms, a perspective with which it's hard to argue. I still have dreams, though, occasionally with Kathy in place of the girl. So, perhaps I'm not as over it as I sometimes think.

Training myself to drive with one hand gave me a sense of control over my life. With the help of modern technology, I became fairly competent at it; nevertheless, my driving in the mountains unnerved Kathy, so I rode shotgun while she drove her luxury sedan out to the northwestern reaches of the county.

Clouds drifted around and among the mountains, hung over peaks, dropped into the valleys, ran along the creek. Steady rain made navigating the gravel road to Queenie's an adventure, causing the car to occasionally lose traction and forcing us to stop a half-dozen times and remove tree limbs from the roadway. I shivered as we crossed Weaver's Creek where we had found the body four years ago.

Sonny, Queenie's yellow lab of indeterminate age, greeted us on the road and barked directions on up to the house. Queenie lounged on her front porch with a cup of coffee in hand, a cardigan sweatshirt over her shoulders.

"Wonderin' when you'd get here."

I squinted at her. "You knew we were coming?"

"These old bones tell me things, Ryder. And Ms. Kathy, you're a sight for sore eyes. Seems forever."

"It has been forever, Queenie. And if it hadn't have been for me this time, Rick would still be back down the mountain drinking his coffee."

"Yeah. He's always been kind of feckless that way. You two ought to invest in a coffee plantation down in Colombia, as much as he drinks the stuff." She held her mug toward us and said, "Speaking of which, this is from a fresh pot. Fetch you some?"

"I'll help bring it out," Kathy offered.

From Queenie's porch, inhaling the clean mountain air while watching the Blue Ridge Mountains disappear through the mist into South Carolina and Georgia, I was reminded why she wanted to preserve this patch of land for future generations.

Queenie returned with a carafe of coffee along with a tray of biscuits and all the fixin's. I waited until we were settled with our vittles before asking what had happened to the professor.

"Wish I knew, Rick. I went down to check on him about two o'clock since he should have been out of here by noon. I'm not a real stickler for time. But SaraJean was gonna come up and clean the place and I didn't want her to have to wait. When we got down there, Sonny knew something was wrong before I did. Took me straight to the storage shed. I could smell it. Oh, sorry. That might not set well with the biscuits."

We assured her it was okay, that we were prepared to deal with the issue of a dead body.

"Anyway, with Sonny was growling at the smell I had idea of what I'd find. Gagged when I opened the door. And there he was, spread out like he was doin' some kind of ritual down there, all spread eagled, face down. Like any good citizen, I called 911. You know I have the sheriff's direct number. I think this one's a pretty good boy. 'Specially compared to that last weasel we had. Anyway, I thought I'd go through standard procedure, not seem like I was looking for anything special. First responders show up, although there's nothing for them to do, 'cept say, 'Yep. He's dead.' Then a deputy comes flyin' down the road, si-reen blarin' like him getting here in a hurry is gonna make a difference. The guy's dead, for Christmas sake. He ain't goin' anywhere. Deputy asks what happened. I tell him just what I told you and twenty minutes later you'd have thought they'd found a nest of Syrian terrorists hidin' out up here. I mean there was every kind of law enforcement vehicle you could imagine." She paused in her monologue. "Need more coffee? Biscuits? I made 'em this morning, knowin' you were comin' up, and all," she said, an impish grin crossing her face. When we declined, she continued.

"So, a'course it wasn't long before I started to get into it with 'em. They had a right to be in the shed and they poked all around. When a detective went into the cabin itself, I followed him, since my experience with those people has given me a rather jaundiced view of their, what shall we say? Integrity? He tells me I have to get out, that this is a crime scene. I tell him the crime scene is obviously the shed. 'Lady,' he says – you know how I love to be called 'lady'—I tell him I am no lady, I'm a woman. This is a new guy, I guess, and nobody's warned him about me. Anyway, he starts in again. 'Ma'am, you did say the deceased was staying here. It is very possible there is evidence in this house that relates to his death. So, unless you want me to arrest you for interfering with a lawful investigation, I suggest you leave. Now.' 'Course, I wanted to argue some more, but decided I really didn't want to be hauled off to the slammer again."

"Well, Queenie," I mused, "with all due respect, I think the guy was right. And I think you exercised laudable restraint."

"I guess. Anyhow, I hung around for a while, keeping an eye on things. Then the detective and the two uniforms who'd gone in there with him come out. Detective has what looks like a pill bottle in a baggie. Gives me a receipt for a bottle of ... let's see, I've got it here somewhere." She poked around in the various pockets of her overalls before extracting a piece of paper. 'Zolpidem. 55 tablets out of a prescription for 90.' Then they blazed their parade back up the drive. Really. Lights flashin' like people needed to get out of their way when there's nobody up here but me. The occasional dead body now and then. Anyway, I thought I'd better follow. Glad I did. They started to come into this house. I drew the line. Said unless they had some reason to suspect I was involved, they weren't coming in here without a warrant. Same for the big barn out back. This time the detective backed down. I'm surprised they haven't been back yet."

"Maybe they're having trouble finding a judge who'll give them what they want."

"I can't believe it would be that hard to find a judge who'd side with them against me."

She looked past us, down the drive leading to her house. "Aw, shit."

"What?" Kathy and I asked in unison.

"Look down the hill. See that?"

Strobing blue and white lights seeped through the mist. A minute later, Brigadoon-like, two squad cars and one unmarked vehicle appeared.

"Don't seem to be in as much of a hurry as they were yesterday," she said. "Although the lights are still pretty egregious."

Sonny had gone down to meet the lawmen. His greeting was vocal and not inviting.

"Ms. Weaver," a man pleaded through the passenger-side window of the unmarked car. "Would you please call your dog off?"

"Oh, my gosh, Detective, he's not gonna hurt you. He's just letting you know how he feels about you being here. Can't imagine where he gets that."

The man, dressed in a khaki summer suit, white shirt with a nondescript necktie, opened the passenger door warily. In the company of the uniformed driver, he came up the steps toward us, four other other uniforms following in their wake while Sonny continued to chastise them.

When Queenie called out, "Sonny, come on up here, boy," the dog hushed and did as commanded.

"Detective Eddington," Queenie said. "So nice to see you again." Turning toward Kathy and me, she added, "Detective, this is Kathy Peters and Rick Ryder. Kathy, Rick, this is Detective Earl Eddington."

Eddington nodded in our direction, then retrieved a piece paper from an inside suit pocket. We all knew Eddington had a search warrant, but Queenie let him go through his litany of presenting it.

"Can I go in the kitchen and get a refill for our coffees?" she asked when he'd finished his presentation.

"You may not. You may come into the house and have a seat but you may not move or so much as touch anything. And the others of you need to stay outside."

Queenie followed him and the four uniformed deputies inside, rolling her eyes as she went, as if to say, See what I have to put up with.

Within five minutes she returned to the porch.

"Don't you want to be in there and keep an eye on them?" I asked.

"Wouldn't do any good. There's six a' them, one a' me. They want to do something underhanded, they're gonna do it. I doubt they will, though, given my recent history with them."

After we'd re-settled ourselves, Kathy asked Queenie, "What were those pills they gave you a receipt for?"

"Zolpidem. Didn't mean anything so I looked it up. A prescription sleeping pill."

"They take anything else?" I asked.

"Not that they let me know about."

"The paper referred to him as 'Pot Professor,'" I said. "Did that have anything to do with why he was in town?"

"The Professor, who shall hereafter be referred to as 'my deceased guest,' was from some school out in Colorado, in town for that medical marijuana get-together at the Sunset View Resort. Supposedly, he was a big researcher. Told me that the conference was getting flak from some of our more enlightened representatives in Raleigh who thought the whole thing was a way to pressure them to legalize it in North Carolina."

"What do you think?"

"I presume most of the people at the conference would be in favor of legalized medical marijuana. You know my feeling on the matter. The resistance to legalizing it at all is ridiculous and to continue to outlaw it for medical use is outrageous if not criminal."

"You know, Queenie," I said, "those views don't endear you to certain people."

"Shoot, Ryder. As I recall, you used to take on corporate polluters, shady developers, and such. Don't remember you backing down from anybody because of who they were."

"That's true. But I always had organizational support behind me. You're just this old lady of the mountains."

"'Just!' she said, her voice rising and her face reddening. She looked at Kathy. "Did he just say 'just?' And 'old?'"

I held my hand up in surrender. "Sorry. That was wrong. But you know what I mean."

"And you think I should quit speakin' my truth?"

"No, Queenie. I'm not saying that at all. Only that you might expect this kind of thing to happen."

"I've been in jail more times than you've been laid in your life—oops, sorry, Kathy ... "

"I get your point, Queenie," Kathy said.

"Yeah. So, don't you be lecturing me about the consequences of my choices. I'm perfectly well aware of them. And the truth is,

I did not know what Marcellus Revis, MD, and PhD by the way, was coming here to do before he got here. He saw my place on the web, liked what he saw and made a reservation. It wasn't 'til he showed up that we realized we were simpatico on the issue."

We could hear the noises of people outside, stomping around the barn. Queenie kept a few goats and chickens, selling milk and eggs to local farm-to-table restaurants. She made some of her own cheese and sold milk to boutique cheese makers. I was amused thinking about what our inquisitors would be stomping around in out there to find something they could use to incriminate our hostess, then recalled that many, probably most, of the county deputies were country boys, used to mucking around in similar quarters.

An hour after they'd arrived, the detective and deputies came to the porch.

"Ms. Weaver. You need to come downtown to give a formal statement. I believe you were advised of that yesterday."

"Yeah, I'll be down. Although I've still not got anything that'll be useful to you fellas."

"I also need to remind you that you aren't to leave the county for the time being."

"You don't have to worry, Detective. I'm not fixin' to go anywhere."

Sonny followed them back to their vehicles, making sure they left.

When they'd gone, Kathy asked her what else she knew of her deceased guest.

"Not much. That school he's with has a big grant to study the noxious weed. He wouldn't say who the money was from. My guess is it's from Big Pharma, people wantin' to be able to trademark products. Those folks aren't high on my list of people doin' good in the world. But the Professor struck me as pretty down-to-earth. I mean he's full of himself and all but I didn't get the idea he was itchin' to make a lot of money. Seemed to me the man liked the work, thought it was important. Struck me as a real scientist."

"Got any thoughts about what may have happened down at the cabin?" Kathy asked.

Queenie's body sagged, as if someone had poked a pin in her, releasing her spirit into the air. She closed her eyes and blinked a few times before she met our eyes again.

"Sorry. It's just that … when I see him in my mind, I also see Stan out there."

"Your former groundskeeper," I said, remembering her longtime employee.

"Yeah. Damn." She pulled a wadded-up tissue out of her overalls and dabbed at her face. "I may have to tear that building down. Hasn't done people much good recently. And, no, I didn't go pokin' around the body to see what had happened. But I doubt it was from natural causes or at his own hands."

"I'm sorry to drag you through this again but do you have any idea who might have benefited from his … demise?"

She shook her head, gazing off into the distance as if it held something that might trigger her memory.

The rain had stopped; clouds were breaking into fat gray patches, lumbering across the sky, late for some pressing celestial event. It smelled of ambrosia. There was also murder in the air.

"Did you notice anything unusual that night after he left your house?" I asked.

"Sonny barked sometime during the night," she said, regaining her composure. "I didn't think much about it. He keeps the bears away and all, leastwise thinks he does. But now when I think back on it, it was a strange bark. Was one of those things happens at night, you know? You hear something, think you might oughta' check it out but don't really want to get of bed?"

"I'm familiar with the feeling," I said.

"Heaven help us if we ever do get broken into," Kathy added. "The dog'll be barking, there'll be all kinds of racket, I'll say, 'Rick, honey. Don't you hear that?' And he'll mumble something and I'll go downstairs and I'll see a U-Haul driving away with all our stuff."

"Yeah," Queenie said. "I'm like that. So, I don't know. Could have been something, you know, suspicious, I guess."

"Did you see him or talk to him other than when he showed up to rent the place?"

"Yeah. I thought you knew. He was here that night before I found him."

My eyes narrowed to slits. My face turned hot. I knew it was red. "How would we have known that?"

"I don't know. Just figured you did."

"My god, Queenie. Do the cops know this?"

"Yeah. I told them when they were here yesterday. Anyway, it was after the first night of the conference, about nine o'clock, he came by. Said he saw the lights on and took a chance I was still up. Now nine is usually pushin' my bedtime, but I've been watching this TV show, based on an Elmore Leonard book, guy's a marshal workin' in West Virginia, anyway, it's like peanuts, can't stop once I start. So, I was in my PJs and a robe when he came to the door. He apologized for bothering me but just wanted to stop and say how much he liked the place. I asked did he want to come in and have a nightcap. He hesitated and I just looked at him like, hey, I'm serious, so he came on in. I poured shots of bourbon for us. He seemed a little edgy but I just chalked that up to his work at the meeting. Not much help, is it?"

"If he was edgy," Kathy said, "maybe he was aware that he was a target. Not necessarily to be killed but that somebody was out to do him some kind of harm."

"That's kinda' what it seemed like, now you've got me thinkin' about it. More worried than keyed up from the day's work. But, like I said, I didn't credit it. If I'd let myself believe he was worried about something, then I'd have had to worry along with him, without even knowing what it was."

A breeze wandered through the pines standing sentry around the house. After a few more minutes of silence, I suggested it was time for us to go since we had other clients to look after.

"I've got some fresh chicken salad and potato salad, you want to stay for lunch."

Simultaneously Kathy and I looked toward the barn.

"No," Queenie said. "I don't eat my own. But there's a cheese maker trades 'em for my goat milk. Free range, cage free, no hormones, write letters home to their folks, all that stuff. Ya eat 'em outta' the supermarket, you forget what the real thing tastes like."

We agreed the clients could wait.

While we were eating, I asked after her neighbors, SarahJean and Arlo Pressley. We'd met them in the course of our previous investigation on the mountain. Arlo was a paraplegic Gulf War vet; SarahJean was his sister and caregiver.

"Seem to be doin' okay. Sarah comes up and helps me with the animals and the garden, cleans the cabin after my guests leave. She keeps her own garden, too, and looks after her brother. Seems to like to be busy. They'd probably enjoy seein' you."

I looked at Kathy and gave a "why not?" shrug.

Queenie called my cell number less than three minutes after we'd left her house.

"Just remembered something," she said. "Don't know if it helps any but I think the sound Sonny and I heard was of someone going by, down toward the guest house. Heard it before the professor stopped by."

"Meaning someone could have been down there to greet him when he arrived that night."

"I guess."

I thanked her and realized that Kathy and I, without anyone formally suggesting it, had become investigators in the case. I told her what Queenie had said.

"So she wasn't in bed when she heard whatever it was. She was up watching that TV show."

"I don't imagine there's much sense in going for a look," I said as we approached the cabin, still surrounded by yellow tape meant to deter people like ourselves.

"Whenever you say something like that I know it's what you want to do."

She turned toward the gravel parking area that fronted the house, pulling in next to a red Jaguar roadster. From the little I knew about vintage cars, I guessed it to be late eighties or early nineties. Other than some road dust, it was immaculate.

"Nice ride," Kathy said.

"Very nice," I agreed. "The professoring business must have been good to him."

We walked around the cabin to the back where the shed was wrapped in the same kind of yellow tape that surrounded the dwelling itself. Beyond the shed was a cleared space about thirty yards deep, planted in grass like that around the cabin.

Beyond the mown grass was woods.

After an unfruitful exploration of the area, I said, "The question is, or at least one question is, why was he in the shed?"

"Curiosity," Kathy stated, matter-of-factly.

"What? You just go wandering into your landlord's property? And then die?"

"Oh, come on. You know you'd go exploring if you were staying in a place like this. Or, maybe he was lured into the shed."

"Lured or directed," I said.

When we got back to the parking area, I gave the Jaguar a once-over. The top was down. If that had been my car, I'd make sure it was closed up for tight. I presumed that the police had searched it and it would soon be in an impound lot, a sad fate for such a lovely vehicle.

SarahJean and Arlo's place was on the other side of the creek from Queenie's property and accessed by a bridge presumably built sometime in the last century. Kathy hesitated before crossing. I told her that on my first visit here, I wasn't sure how safe it was, either, until I saw a pickup truck in the yard. If that vehicle could make it across, I reasoned, so could ours.

SaraJean was outside to greet us before we'd parked the car. A pretty woman, nearing forty, I supposed. Blond hair pulled into a pony tail. Blue jeans. Plaid shirt worn open over a white T-shirt. Rugged boots. A country girl, spiritual daughter to the Queenie Weavers of the world.

"Well, if it isn't the famous investigators, Rick Ryder and Kathy Peters. Ain't you a sight for sore eyes?"

Following a round of hugs, she said, "I'd like to think you came all this way to see us, but I suspect you've been up to see Queenie."

Kathy, the family diplomat, said, "If fact we were. But we couldn't come all this way and not drop in on you and Arlo."

"Well, let's go see that good-for-nothing wastrel of a brother."

A man in a wheelchair was in the living room, a blanket covering him from the waist down. He turned his attention away from the TV toward us.

"Your sister has just described you in the most glowing terms," I said.

"Ryder, you ol' whore. C'mon in." He turned his motorized vehicle to face us. "And Ms. Peters."

His grin was infectious.

"Now, I know Rick is one of them re-covering folk and keeps it on the straight and narrow, but Ms. Kathy, can I interest you in sharing some of God's own finest medicine. This stuff," he said, holding up a baggie of greenish-brown plant material which had been in his lap, "comes to us today from Colorado. It's got a wonderful name which, because I have been enjoying its salutary effects, I cannot for the life of me remember."

"Arlo," his sister said, "you do not have to offer your dope to everyone who comes in the door. Not everyone appreciates it, you know."

"Ah, but these folks are not just 'everyone,' dear sister. These are the Peters and Ryder of investigatory fame." He turned back toward Kathy. "Are you not?"

"Yes, we are, Arlo, and I do appreciate the offer, but I'm afraid I, too, shall have to decline."

"I understand, I understand. I really do. If I hadn't had the lower part of my body shot off while defending democracy in parts of the world that had never heard the word much less expressed an interest in practicing it, I might be as reluctant as you are to indulge in the evil weed. Perhaps I can look at my condition as a blessing. Sit, sit. Stay a spell. And of course all of that peroration was bullshit. I've been gettin' high since I was fourteen, but it is the only thing that keeps the devil away nowadays. A whole lot better than heavy pain meds and anti-depressants."

"Glad to see you're still your old self," I said.

"Well, who else's old self would I be? Hey! You know what I'm fixin' to do. Gonna put Fantasia on the DVD player. You remember Fantasia, that far-out Disney movie? You know it is speculated that old Walt used the weed himself, and very likely LSD. Didn't know that, did you? Anyway, gonna pop that in the player and do a couple of hits of this Colorado herb. Should be a fun afternoon. You oughta join me."

"Arlo!"

"It's okay, little sister. They know I'm just havin' fun. Although, I am serious about what I'm going to do. Didn't really expect you'd come along. After all, y'all are professionals, right."

It was the first time I'd heard an edge to Arlo's voice, like this might not be as much fun as he made it out to be.

"I presume you know that Queenie's caught up in something again, don't you?" I asked.

"Oh, my gosh," SaraJean said. "What's happened now?"

"I'm surprised you don't know already," I said and quickly told her what had happened.

"Do they think she had anything to do with it?" SaraJean asked, eyes wide open.

"I doubt it. But I imagine there are parties in the county who will try to make her as uncomfortable as they can. In fact, they've already started."

"So, Ryder?" Arlo injected. "Why are you involved in this?"

"Queenie called this morning to make sure we knew what was going on so we thought we'd come on out and check on things. More like friends than detectives. And of course, once we got here, we let ourselves get sucked into it. So, since we're here, might as well ask if either of you noticed any unusual comings or going up and down this road two nights ago?"

SarahJean said she hadn't. "'Course, I sleep pretty good here. The creek running by is like someone singin' you a lullaby. Arlo, on the other hand ... "

"Yeah, I pretty much don't sleep, not like regular people. I nod off in the chair for fifteen, twenty minutes at a time. That's about it. On the other hand, as my sister is wont to point out, I do get to rest a lot. But in answer to your question, I'm pretty sure this is true and not a dream—I often go out onto the bridge of a night, sit and listen, like SarahJean, to the creek. If it's moonlit, that's even better. Moonshine off the water, that'll make you forget your problems."

After a pause when it seemed he'd forgotten the question on the table, I asked, "And what happened the other night?"

"Oh, yeah. It was quiet, like I said. I did say that, didn't I? I heard a car coming down the road. Now you know, that road is not heavily traversed. People goin' to see Queenie go up and down the other side of the ridge. There's the occasional car comin' from over towards Tennessee, but you don't hardly see nobody out here at night. Piqued my curiosity you might say. Whoever it was wasn't speedin' but they weren't dawdlin' either. I turned my chair to look directly across the creek. Did you know I was a spotter in the Army? Damned good one, I might add. I know how to look, even in the dark, and it was kind of a semi-lit night, the kind you like on Halloween, just a little spooky." He squeezed his eyes shut, remembering. "Well, anyways, at first I couldn't see anything except it seemed like something was moving through my field of vision. As it got closer, I realized it was a truck, small one, a pickup, like maybe an F-150."

"Like yours," I said.

"Just like it, I think."

"I don't suppose you could you see the plate? Or the color?"

"Nah. Not from down here."

"What time was that?" Kathy asked.

"Ten, ten-thirty. Maybe a little later. You understand, me and time have a somewhat mutable relationship."

"Got that," Kathy agreed. "But it would fit with Queenie's story of the professor coming by her place for a drink at nine, hanging around for a bit before heading to the cabin. Someone could have been waiting for him."

Arlo said, "Maybe you've found your bad guy, or guys."

"Hardly found," I demurred. "But it's a little bit to go on, anyway."

"And speaking of going on," Kathy said, "it's about time we did, don't you think, Rick?"

I did. We gave well-wishes, said goodbyes. SaraJean accompanied us as far as the bridge.

"He seems a little grumpier than I remember," I said. "I mean, he's a pretty dark guy, but he almost snarled back there."

"Yeah," SarahJean agreed. "I think the novelty of not having legs has pretty much worn off. Most days he's pretty good. And the pot does help. It's just that he can't do anything, you know. And has no interest in getting involved with the VA or anything organized."

Kathy said, "You're an angel to take care of this place and him and help Queenie out."

"Thanks for saying that. But I'm no volunteer at Queenie's. She pays me $15.00 an hour. Says that's what the minimum wage ought to be and she's by God gonna pay it. And she's fun to be around so it's not like real work at all."

It was well on to mid-afternoon. The sky reneged on its promise to clear up. No rain but the clouds had turned dark, ominous. While Kathy was maneuvering us down the mountain to the four-lane, I called Nate and was surprised when the man himself answered.

"Lose your help, Counselor?" I asked.

"Nah. You know I couldn't chase her out of here if I wanted to. And I sure, by God, don't want to. I would be up a creek. So, Counselor, waz up?"

Back when I first met Nate and he discovered I was a lawyer as well as an investigator, he began calling me "Counselor" and I always reciprocated. It was now a thing between us.

"Been out to Queenie's. Seems the old gal's embroiled in another skirmish with the gendarmes."

"Has a knack for it, doesn't she? I don't really think there's much to do right now. As I understand it, they haven't arrested her or anything. Just taking the opportunity to harass her."

I told him about Queenie's late-night visit from the professor and the vehicle that Queenie thought she'd heard and that Arlo said he'd seen."

"Interesting stuff of uncertain value. And, as I intimated, I don't have a client here. Just to keep things clear, if you're working on a case involving her, you're working for her, not me. You'll probably want to see the autopsy and the toxicology reports. Even then, it may all be moot. At least as far as Queenie's concerned."

"I believe she wants to see justice done, Nate."

"Oh, that. I think I heard some talk about it in law school. And right now all you have is a corpse. No suspects. And for all the grief Queenie gets, I doubt she's gonna wind up in trouble over this. But my eyes and ears downtown will keep me up to date with what's happening in the case of this pot professor. I'll let you know if I hear anything."

"How are things with our sometime employer," Kathy asked after I'd disconnected.

"Nate's Nate. Doesn't seem to think there's anywhere for this case to go."

"Maybe he's right. Maybe there is no case. This guy died after too much booze and pills. Case closed."

"Maybe. But I'm with Queenie. I think there's more to it. Nate said there are no suspects. But how does he know that?"

"Are there?"

"I don't know. But we haven't looked into it to see who all is out there lurking in the underbrush."

"'Lurking in the underbrush'?"

"A figure of speech."

"If someone out there might be a suspect, but we don't know about them, are they really a suspect?"

"The 'tree falling in the woods' thing?"

"Precisely."

"I wonder if Nate's been talking to the sheriff's people, if that's where he got the idea that there aren't any suspects. If so, that simply means that the sheriff's department is not investigating anyone."

There's a Tuesday night AA meeting at a Presbyterian church on the north side of town. One of the first things I'd done when I moved to Asheville fifteen years ago was get myself to a meeting. I don't go daily as many of the old-timers do. I attend frequently, if sporadically, and I like to know where and when the meetings are for those times when I feel a meeting will do me good. It's also the place where I met the man who would become—other than Kathy—my best friend.

The first time I attended this meeting, a huge bear of a man stood up and said, "I'm Nate. I'm an alcoholic."

At certain AA meetings, a member stands in the front of the room and tells their story. Nate told his. A big, smart, black kid from a middle-class family. All-State football team. Brown University on a scholarship in the era before Affirmative Action entered our vocabulary and racism was not nearly as politically incorrect as it is now. Feels the weight of extraordinary expectations. Gets in fights. Begins drinking. (Unlike my story in which I began to drink and then got into fights.) Made it through law school at Chapel Hill with honors, fueled by alcohol and Dexedrine. Clerked for a state Supreme Court judge. Got a couple of DUIs. Came home to the mountains and got involved in the civil rights struggle. After another DUI and embarrassing his family deeply, relatives encouraged him to get more involved with church. A counselor suggested AA. Unlike the church, AA worked.

He's still sober and doesn't talk about it. Although, in addition to the standard framed diplomas and photos with him and various dignitaries that hang on the walls of his office, he also has a prominent photo of himself in an orange jumpsuit and handcuffs. Says it helps cut the bullshit with some of his clients. He shows up at a meeting two or three times a year, "just to remind myself what it's all about," and he tells me our Monday morning meetings are his "regular" AA.

As expected, he wasn't at this meeting but my sponsor was. "Jim W." He wandered over while I was setting up chairs.

"How're things?"

"Other than that business is a little slow, things are good."

"You don't have to wait until things go south to call me, you know. Sponsors do like to hear about the good things that are happening."

"Yes, Jim. I'll work on that."

After the meeting, he asked if I wanted to join him and a couple other old-timers for coffee. I knew that among the others would be a guy called Snook. Snook was one of those "meeting-a-day" folks, which was fine with me, except he proselytized the idea wherever he was, which would include over coffee after a meeting. I declined.

A crack of thunder woke us followed quickly by Audrey, our boy dog with the girl's name, leaping onto the bed. The bedside clock showed 11:52. An explosion of lightning lit up the room. A sucker for dramatic weather, I put on slippers and went downstairs where I could keep a better eye on things. Living in semi-isolation as we do, security lights illuminate both the front and back yards. I opened the glass doors for a better look. The smell of ozone and the funk of wet woods filled my nostrils. For a while the rain sliced through the light, almost parallel to the ground. Occasionally, after a bright flash and before the following thunder, I heard the loud crack of a lightning-struck tree snapping. The next day we would see its charred remains.

Two

The Following Monday

Storms came and went the rest of the week and through the weekend. I had to clear debris from the drive before I could get out to meet Nate. In the area around the Downtown Bakery, like all of the city center, parking was at a premium. I availed myself of a handicapped-designated space within a half block of the café to the annoyance of others as I walked, unaided, to my destination.

When I arrived Nate, as usual, was holding court in a booth, chatting up the cute waitress.

"Good timing," he said as I approached. He turned to the young woman. "I believe my man here will have a cup of coffee."

I agreed, adding an orange-cranberry scone to the order.

"Pretty girl," I said, after she'd gone. "Recruiting interns?"

"We are allowed to enjoy the beauty with which God has blessed our lives. In fact, He would be disappointed with us if we didn't."

"So we can ogle at will, is that it?"

"One must be respectful. Drooling is not permitted, for instance."

"Good to know the rules. And speaking of rules, I suppose it's too soon to have heard about lab reports concerning the recent unfortunateness up at Queenie's."

"Yes, it is. But Katrina has started hounding the coroner's office."

"You don't have any standing in this, do you?"

"You mean what gives my office leave to badger the coroner?"

"Something like that."

"I am Queenie Weaver's personal attorney. And even if she has not engaged me to look into this specific case, she has had her property and her home searched and herself questioned in regard to Dr. Revis's untimely demise. My client has a right to know when this investigation will be concluded and she will not have to concern herself with further harassment. By the way, have we talked about you being on the clock for your work on this?"

"During our last conversation, you made it clear we were on our own if we were going to take up the case."

"Consider yourselves on my ticket now for anything you do related to Ms. Queenie Weaver and the case of the slain professor."

"Could be a book title in there."

"Just in case this thing goes south on us and Queenie is implicated in any way, why don't you do some preliminary research on the guy?"

We went on to discuss the issues of the day, whether or not the republic could withstand the assaults by the new administration and the nonsensical things our representatives in Raleigh kept foisting upon us. After an hour, Nate said he had to leave to meet a bona fide client.

He leaned forward, making what was to follow feel intimate. "Just to give you an idea of the kind of stuff the people I represent have to put up with, this kid, fourteen, gets into a scuffle in school. Of course, the other kid is white, lives in

North Asheville. My client—actually, the son of my client; we'll get to that—the kid gets in-school suspension for two weeks. Not out of line for that kind of thing. Except that my client, the kid's father, finds out that nothing happened to the other kid. No suspension. Nada. Father goes to the schoolhouse, asks to talk to the principal. Principal's not available. When will he be? Don't know. Okay, I'll wait. An hour goes by and of course the steam is building up inside of him. He says, okay, let me see an assistant principal. Not available. When will he be? Et cetera. You might see where this is goin'. He starts to get loud. Swears at the secretary or whoever is behind the desk. 'God damn, I want to talk to someone about what has happened to my son.' Gets the, 'Sir, you're going to have to calm down.' Which is like throwing gasoline on the fire. Pretty soon the school resource officer shows up. According to my client, he's gotten himself calmed down but keeps repeating that he wants to talk to someone about what has happened to his son or at least make an appointment to do so. He is adamant. The resource officer tells him he going to have to leave the school campus. Then he really goes off. Doesn't hit anyone, nothing physical, but the resource officer calls for backup. He gets escorted off campus in handcuffs and taken to the po-lice station where he is charged with disturbing the peace, refusing to comply with a lawful order, et cetera. That's my world, counselor."

I felt for him. I knew the vagaries and vicissitudes of institutional bias as well as he did. I said, rather sardonically, "Maybe something'll turn up with Queenie's situation and you can come to the aid, once again, of an elderly white country woman."

He leaned back in the booth. "Be a breath of fresh air."

I fed the parking meter and took myself for a walk around downtown enjoying the cleared-out atmosphere. Before I'd returned to the car, Kathy showed in my phone's little window.

"Want to grab lunch?"

It seemed like I'd just had breakfast, but in fact Nate and I had managed to use up the better part of two hours solving our own and the world's problems. Although we knew that we weren't in charge of everything, we did believe that if people only listened to us, we'd all be better off.

I texted back, "What did you have in mind?"

A new taco place had opened just outside downtown. It promised homemade tortillas and, what was now de rigueur in the area, "locally sourced ingredients." The farm-to-table movement had not simply arrived in Asheville, it had landed like a tsunami. The restaurant was one of those semi-fast food places where you stand in line to order, they hand you a number so they can locate you, you find your own table and they bring your food when it's ready. She said she'd meet me there in ten minutes.

While I was working on—at least thinking about—Queenie's dead professor, Kathy had taken the lead on another case we'd recently acquired. Caesar Marotti, a well-knows local businessman of less-than-squeaky-clean repute, suspected his wife of having an affair with the head of a competing firm. He wasn't as concerned about infidelity as he was about corporate secrets being compromised. Ryders and Peters job was to confirm or refute his suspicions. Ordinarily, for safety reasons, Kathy and I tailed people as a duo. We also thought people were likely to be less wary of a couple they kept seeing than they would be of a single person. In this instance, however, Kathy took it on herself to follow the woman.

"She shops a lot," Kathy said after we'd found seats.

"That's it?"

"It's only the first morning. But she's been down to Biltmore Village, out to the mall, downtown. All in three hours. It's what you do when you're looking to buy something specific."

"But no other man or a place where she might rendezvous with someone?"

"Nope. She met a couple of other women right before I called you. They were going into Arthur's."

Arthur's was another new restaurant like many of the other new restaurants, the kind that you knew—without ever taking a step inside—would have edamame and kale on the menu.

"You going to try to pick up the tail after we eat?"

"I'll check the parking garage where she left her car. If it's still there, I'll follow her some more."

"And if not?"

"Guess I'll go home. Do some checking on those internet dating cases."

These had become our bread and butter, people wanting background checks on potential internet dates. It didn't require licensed private detectives to do this work. For a fee, anyone willing to take the time could access the same sites we searched. But the people who wanted our service found it easier to hire the work out. More than thirty percent of the people we checked had questionable pasts, criminal histories, or serious bad debt problems. Several turned out not be the person they presented themselves as being at all, like the guy who said he'd been a preacher at a church that never existed, or the woman who claimed she'd been a university professor but was unknown by the college she said she'd taught at. With that work and investigating the occasional murder, we kept busy—busy enough, at least, for semi-retired people.

Tacos were on the cusp of becoming a cliché in town.

But when were finished with the meal, we were happy to add this to our menu of affordable eateries. Made-on-the-premises tortillas tasted like food, not something packaged in plastic or cardboard. The fillings were fresh as advertised. Not a leaf of kale in sight.

We smooched a little in the parking lot before Kathy headed toward the parking deck where she'd last seen our client's wife. I took off the other way to my favorite bookstore cum coffee shop. It was two blocks from a city garage where the first hour of parking came free and didn't involve parallel parking—inevitably a challenge for a one-handed driver.

In the café, a row of stools stood parallel to a counter overlooking the street, offering a vantage from which to observe the passing scene. I ordered an herbal iced tea, grabbed one of the two unoccupied seats and plugged in my laptop.

A search for Marcellus Revis, MD and PhD, brought up ten-plus pages of entries. The first several were news accounts of his death in papers from New York to San Francisco and, of course, scores of internet comments. There was his bio from East Colorado State University, which included having doctorates in psychopharmocology and ethnopharmocology as well as a medical degree. At East Colorado, he researched the medicinal properties of marijuana. He was a fellow of the relevant national boards and a member of the board of directors of a prominent national marijuana law reform organization.

His personal website revealed little additional information other than some photos of him in various poses with three vintage Jaguars captioned with the information that he was a member of the Rocky Mountain Jaguar Club. In every photo he wore a tan suit over a black crew-neck shirt, his white hair pulled into a pony tail. He identified no other interests or hobbies.

The bulk of the remaining internet entries were for papers, books, and articles he had written, along with citations by others of his work. He was clearly a leader in his field and an obvious pick to be the keynote speaker at a conference about the medical uses of marijuana. What wasn't obvious was why anyone would want to murder him—if murder was, indeed, what had occurred that night at the cabin. I kept scrolling and surfing to see what might pop up. Like workplace supervisors who follow the philosophy of "managing by walking around," detectives engage in what others might see as aimless, non-directed behavior. While doing that, I came across an interesting headline: "Pot professor accused of plagiarism." Nice alliteration, I thought. In a Denver newspaper article published six years previously, two scientists at another university had accused Dr. Revis of using information they had published earlier without their permission or acknowledgment. As with many similar entries on the internet, there was no easily found follow-up. It seemed to indicate that the professor, while having a kind of celebrity status, had not always been held in the best regard by all his peers.

A Wikipedia piece was the only other item to claim my attention during my hour-and-a-half trip into the ether world (though I admit some of that time was hijacked by the parade of kooks, shoppers, buskers, homeless people, and a few gorgeous women strolling by the window). It noted that Dr. Revis had been married for a time to Anne McDonald of Celo, NC, and that they had a son, Marcus Revis, Jr. I found no other mention of either of those two.

The Celo reference was particularly interesting. The town, about forty miles north of Asheville, was founded as an "intentional community" in the late 1930s and was an early draw for some of the kinds of people who would later become referred to as "hippies," although in contemporary photos it would be hard to tell the current residents from any other middle-class, mostly white folks. I wondered if Anne and the professor ever lived there together. Then I wondered when the professor's interest in marijuana began and if he had been living in western North Carolina at the same time that Queenie was gaining local notoriety in the early 1970s.

My back was letting me know that I'd spent enough time on a seat that didn't support it. I packed up and returned to the parking garage. Once in the car, the engine running, I enunciated, "Dial Queenie." My wish was its command.

"Ryder. What can I do you for?"

"So, my dear. The other day you gave the impression that you had never met Professor Revis before he came to stay in your guest house. Is that true?"

A pregnant pause swelled.

"Is it true that I gave that impression or is it true that I'd never met him before?"

"The latter."

After another, briefer, pause she said, "I guess you better come on out again."

Kathy answered her phone after several rings. "Hold on a minute, Rick."

She got back to me in less than that. "It turns out Ms. Marotti also enjoys good beer."

"And you know this how?"

"That's only an assumption, actually. I just now followed her into the Parched Brother."

This was a downtown bar featuring Belgian ales and local brews.

"Is that where you are now?"

"I came outside when the phone rang. Before I did, though, I was able to see her walk to a table in a dark corner at the back of the room."

"The perfect assignation spot. Did she meet someone?"

"I don't think anyone was there when she arrived. But a guy just went down the stairs. I want to go back and see if he's joined her."

"Okay. I'm going back out to Queenie's. I'll fill you in over dinner."

Since that first case we worked on with Queenie, whenever I cross the bridge over Weaver Creek on the way to her house, the image of a young man's body floating at the bottom of a waterfall revisits me. Nonetheless, I stopped on the bridge and closed my eyes, hearing only the water scrabbling below before disappearing into the woods. If not for the memories it conjured, this would be an idyllic spot. I took a deep breath and drove on.

Sonny came to greet me the way he welcomes everyone who approaches his mistress's home. He's more welcoming to some than to others and we had gotten to know each other over the years. He made a lot of noise, but his tail was about to shake loose his hind end. Queenie sat on the porch, a glass of brown liquid in her hand. I assumed it was tea. The hard stuff would come later.

"So, Ryder, you been doin' some snoopin'," she said as I climbed the steps.

"Yeah, Queenie. That's pretty much what I do, what you have even paid me for."

"Want somethin' to wet your whistle while we talk about it?"

I did.

"Pull yourself up a chair. I'll be right back."

I watched as white clouds billowed from the west and jostled for space on an azure field. During the dark days of my misspent youth, I took drugs to achieve that kind of vision. On this day I wouldn't have to worry about who was driving or where I'd parked the car. This was better.

Queenie returned with a tray holding two glasses, a pitcher of tea, a bowl of ice, and lemon wedges. Each glass held a sprig of mint. We leaned toward each other and clinked glasses.

"Found something interesting, I take it."

"Not so much found something as had some questions raised. Such as, how likely was it that this guy who married a woman from Celo, known at the time as the hippie capital of the mountains, would not know the hippie queen of Buncombe County? Especially since both of you had an interest in marijuana. As I recall, back in the day you were teaching people how to grow it. I know Celo is not right around the corner, but it's not that far away either. And this guy turns out to have an abiding, continuing interest in the plant. You might imagine that my curiosity was piqued."

"How's the tea?" she asked.

"Very good."

"Yeah. It's my special blend. Let it brew in the sun. Don't worry. Nothin' illegal in it."

"Yes. It's good tea. Sooo ... the professor?"

"Marcellus Revis, MD, PhD, etc. Yes, our paths did cross back in the day. Oh, jeez. I don't know how much of this I want to replay. It's been a long time, you know."

We sat in silence, enjoying—at least, I was enjoying—the surroundings. I tilted my head to the breeze like a dog does when you blow in its face. I was in no hurry. Nor was Queenie.

Finally she started to murmur at me.

"You know I grew up on this land, in this house. Was a student at Chapel Hill when my parents died. I was twenty years old and came home to take care of the place."

Her voice took on a reminiscent tone. "It was 1960 and marijuana had begun to show up on college campuses around the country. It'd been around for a long time, of course, but it was very underground. That was still the time of the Beat Generation. The hippies didn't come until later, the mid-sixties. A bunch of us at school were all into Allen Ginsburg and Burroughs and Kerouac. You weren't hip if you hadn't read On the Road and Howl and Naked Lunch." She almost smiled.

"Anyway, I was home tryin' to take care of this place and a guy I'd met at the university came up here one day. He knew I'd smoked weed back in Chapel Hill and he had some—a bunch, really—and he talked about me growing it up here. Ideal conditions. Out of the way. He thought I could make a lot of money at it. We talked. He told me about people who had experience growing it. He hung around for a while and boys being boys and girls being girls, well, you know. He was smart. I mean real smart. You could tell he was going somewhere and probably in academia. He had that kind of mind.

"I think you pretty well know the rest of the story. About me anyway. That all came out after that college kid died at the falls."

I remembered the stories of how Queenie started growing her own, although she claimed she never made any money at it. What was profitable was teaching other people how to grow it. She taught classes up here, all very hush-hush, word of mouth kind of stuff. People left "love offerings" for her—food, pottery, money, beads, whatever. She gave that up when someone approached her on the street in Asheville, someone she didn't know but who recognized her, and asked her when her next classes were. It was no longer an underground sort of thing.

"You were lovers," I said, returning to the professor.

"It was a fling. I don't think either one of us thought it would continue once he got off the mountain although we did stay in contact, on and off. You know, the occasional post card from somewhere. Then the internet arrived and we started keeping up that way."

"So when this conference came up ... "

"Yeah. So when it came up, it seemed only natural to ask him if he wanted to stay here."

"Not to get too personal, but why was he down at the cabin and not up at the house?"

She said nothing for a minute while she looked at me.

"You may have noticed that I have lived up here a long time by myself. Like it. Not that I don't like company now and then. So long as you don't overstay your welcome. You get one meal or a couple of drinks. That's it. So the question of whether or not he would stay here

arose. I heard that he also keeps – kept – strange hours, although he wasn't here long enough for me to see that."

"That's a nice car he was driving."

"He was always into sports cars. Drove an old MG at Chapel Hill."

"Did his family have money?"

"I don't know. He didn't talk about them. He always seemed to have some, though." She was quiet again before turning toward me. "How does all of this help you understand what happened down at the cabin?"

"I have no idea. Good chance it has nothing to do with it. But ... "

"I know, Ryder. Like you're always sayin', 'you never know.'"

"'And so it goes.'"

We sat and rocked in silence a while like two old-timers whilin' away the late afternoon. I suppose one of use should have been whittling for it to have been a perfect picture.

"Do you have any ideas about this?" I asked, breaking the spell.

"Nothin'. I think I told you, there was a lot of money involved in what he was doing. I know there were people putting money into his lab hopin' it would lead to patents on medicines. But I can't figure why anyone would want to kill him over it."

"Queenie. You're not that naïve. People get killed when there's a lot of money involved. And I believe we're talkin' about a lot of money. Maybe someone else is doing similar research. Thought Marcus might get to something before they did and he, or the company that was funding him, would get the big bucks. Who knows? Maybe one of his colleagues, or a student he was working with."

An idea floated, drifted unbidden into my mind, as is supposed to be the case when we snoops do what we do. "You know anybody out there? In Colorado? Anybody involved in the pot scene?"

"As I understand it, Ryder, t'ain't anybody in Colorado these days who isn't involved in the pot scene."

"Touché."

Silence overtook us again. There are places around with views just as nice as the one from Queenie's front porch, but there was something about the feel of that place that I'd not found anywhere else. It would be hard for me to get anything done if I lived up there. I'd be inclined to sit in a rocking chair all day and watch whatever show the heavens chose to put on. I also understood why someone might kill to not lose this property.

"You're wonderin' why I didn't tell you all this before," she said, breaking into my reverie.

"The question occurred to me."

"You do remember that the fact that I knew the boy who died at the waterfalls was all the law needed for them to arrest me for his murder. God only knows what they'll do if they find out I knew the professor."

"I understand, Queenie, but don't you think they'll find out anyway?"

"You have a high opinion of their investigative skills."

"Realistic," I said. "After all, I found out."

"I dunno. It all seems so, what? Far-fetched. World famous biologist from Colorado, in favor of making marijuana legal for medical purposes, comes to a conference in Asheville, North Carolina and is found dead in a cabin in the mountains. Dead from unknown causes. Just dead. Why? I don't get it."

That brief statement reminded me that we didn't know by what means the professor came to his untimely end. Suicide? Heart attack? Killed in a way that left no indication that something had been done to him?

"What about the sleeping pills?" I asked.

"What about them?"

"Maybe he overdosed on them, them and alcohol. How much did he have to drink at your house?"

"Shot of bourbon."

"A shot?"

"Well, a stiff shot. But still, only one. Not like we sat around boozin'."

"We don't know if they found alcohol down at the cabin. And what about the sleeping pills? Could he have overdosed on those?"

"And then wandered into the shed?"

I shrugged. "Instead of engaging in idle speculation we could wait until Nate gets ahold of the autopsy and toxicology reports."

"Could, I suppose. But, at my age, idle speculation is one of life's great pastimes."

The sun had drifted to the west and was about to descend below the edge of the porch's roof-line, letting me know it was time to take my leave.

"You know, Ryder," Queenie said. "This isn't even a case yet. Remind me again why you're spendin' all this time on it."

"I guess because it's more interesting than investigating the backgrounds of people involved in Internet dating. I'm always surprised when I meet a couple who met that way and who've stayed together a while given the high proportion of psychos we've come across."

I called out Kathy's number again before I drove away. She said she'd stayed at the bar long enough for two glasses of white wine, told the bartender she guessed she'd been stood up, and left. The woman and the man were still ensconced in the corner of the room.

"I assume there's something going on and I wanted to get a better look at the guy, but I didn't think I could just sit there not drinking and I didn't want to drink anymore. I'd never have gotten home. Fortunately, I found a parking space in that lot across the alley. That's where I am now, hoping they'll come out before too long."

***

The menagerie back on Cove Road expressed mixed feelings about having been abandoned by their people most of the day. Audrey, of course, was beside himself, as if he couldn't believe his good luck that I'd returned. The cats, on the other hand, expressed their disdain for my cavalier attitude toward their meal time by sulking until after I'd put their food out and had left the kitchen.

Kathy's call came immediately after I'd taken a glass of tonic and lime to the deck. I'd picked up a rotisserie chicken from one of the "healthy food" supermarkets and ripped half of it apart. How you do this with one hand is to take a big carving fork and skewer one end of the carcass to the cutting board, then pull away at it. I turned it into a curried chicken salad, threw together some greens, poured a glass of Pinot Grigio for the missus, and left it all in the fridge. With my own drink refreshed, I was back on the deck when she arrived home.

"You love going out there, don't you," she said as she sipped her pre-dinner libation.

"I do. If I were a writer, I'd love to write her biography. One hesitates to say they don't make 'em like her anymore. I'm sure there are equally interesting contemporary women. But you have to admit she is one of a kind."

"Do you think she has anything else to hide, in addition to the fact that she'd known the guy and didn't bother to pass that on to the law?"

"I don't know. And I don't blame her. Her experience with 'the law' hasn't been, how shall we say, conducive to candor."

"I understand. But what happens when they find out? Won't that make things worse?"

"Could. But she's counting on their collective incompetence."

"Kind of risky, don't you think?"

"Risky is not a deterrent to Queenie."

Kathy rolled her eyes. "I love the woman, too. How can you not? But I think she leans on the idea that she doesn't have to follow the rules that the rest of us do."

"Ready for chicken salad?" I asked, moving the subject away from Queenie.

After dinner, we walked up in the woods following paths along the creek. Audrey kept us company, making sure we didn't fall in. The cats could not have been less interested. They knew these woods better that any of the rest of us, their nocturnal predations taking them places we would never go.

We avoided any talk of work on the way up the hill, enjoying the twilight sounds of the creek and birds and twittering insects. On our return, we relapsed as Kathy asked what I thought might have happened out at Queenie's.

"I have no idea. A couple of things are curious, though. The fact that Queenie did know the guy and didn't tell the cops does raise some questions."

"You think she might have done it?"

"I don't. Can't see a motive. And besides, I can't imagine Queenie doing someth—"

"Isn't that the kind of thing family and neighbors always say," Kathy snapped, "when someone goes off and commits some foul act, you know, mass killings, that kind of thing?" She switched to a falsetto voice. "I just can't imagine Jim Bob doin' somethin' like that."

"I know. We get in trouble when we underestimate the kinds of things people are actually capable of. But Queenie? Really?"

"Okay. Ruling out Queenie—for now—you said that there were a couple of things that are curious. What's the other?"

"Well, the car—or truck—that Queenie heard and Arlo

saw. What was it doing up there?"

"Maybe a friend of the professor or someone he'd met at the conference came to visit."

"This imagined person drives up there before the professor arrives, stays for the professor to show up, then leaves soon after? That's if Arlo's recollection of the time he saw the car is accurate."

"This is a man who smokes pot all day. You're counting on his memory being accurate?"

"Yeah, well. ... "

Three

Wednesday

S ee the paper, Ryder?"

"And good morning to you, Queenie. As a matter of fact, no, I haven't."

"Sleepin' in, huh?"

"No, Ms. Weaver, I've not been sleeping in. I just finished my morning exercise, had a shower, and, before you rang, had sat down with a cup of coffee and our local bird-cage liner. I've only scanned the front page. Apparently, there's something inside that would have caught my attention had I gotten that far."

"You wanna come out and feed the chickens, milk the goats, and then compare the arduousness of our mornings?"

"Okay. I've turned the page. And I see a headline. *Death of noted biologist and proponent of medical marijuana ruled a suicide.* That, perchance, what's gotten you so fired up this a.m.?" I glanced at the story as I spoke to her. *Medical Examiner: Toxicology report reveals high levels of sleeping pills and alcohol.*

"Boy. Once you wake up, Ryder, you're quick as a whip."

"Yeah. Hard to get anything past me after I get going. How come we didn't hear about this from Nate? You don't suppose he's losing his edge down there do you?"

"I doubt that. More like his attention's been elsewhere."

I remembered his story about the father he was representing.

"What's got you so riled up? I would've thought you'd be relieved. You're off the hook. Not that you were ever really on it."

"It's wrong, that's what. That man did not commit suicide."

"Someone faked the tox report?"

"Beats me. But that man was at the top of his game, Rick. He was absolutely basking in his notoriety. After the gig here, he was going up to do the same thing in Ohio. He was also pretty high on himself for the clinical work he was doing, finding possible cures for things. And the man didn't drink."

That last sentence was disorienting.

"You told me that you two drank together."

"One drink, Rick. He was very clear about that. And he told me about the sleeping pills. Said he only took them when he was traveling, when his time clock got twisted around. But given the work he was doing, he had to be cleaner than Caesar's wife. Squeaky clean. Because there are people out to make him look bad, people who are against the whole idea of medical marijuana, afraid it will lead to legalizing it outright."

"That's not an unreasonable concern although hardly a reason to kill someone. I mean, who are we talking about here? The DEA?"

"Do you have any idea how many people would lose their jobs if marijuana were legalized? It's already happening. Fewer people go to prison on pot charges. Less need for guards. Less need for beds. Less need for prisons. Look at the prison guards' union in California. They're going nuts over this. Although there are cops who say they like the idea 'cause then they can focus on the 'hard' drug traffic."

I could hear the quotation marks around 'hard' in her tone of voice.

"You don't believe it."

"Hell, Rick. It would nice to think that, and that's one of the selling points for legalization. But the reality is, the cops like chasing pot. There's so much of it, it's like shooting fish in a barrel for them."

"Okay. I'll stipulate to all that. But come on, Queenie, do you think there's been a conspiracy among law enforcement types to take the professor out?"

"I don't know. What I do know is that the man I spoke to the other night was not a man on the verge of suicide."

I remembered my conversation with Kathy in regards to making assumptions about what individuals were capable of.

As if she'd been reading my mind, Queenie said, "I know what you're thinkin', Rick. You never know what any one person might do. But there is no way Marc Revis was going to kill himself that night."

"Alright, Queenie. Say you're right—"

"I'm right."

"Stipulated. Now what?"

"I want someone to find out what really happened."

"And who might that someone be?"

"Come on, Rick. Don't be obtuse."

"Peters and Ryder Private Detective Agency, by any chance?"

"Jeez," Queenie said, frustration radiating from her voice. "Lemme talk to Kathy. She's awake, isn't she?"

"Yes. And this conversation has delayed my delivery of her tea."

"You do that? Take her tea in the morning?"

"I do."

"Prince of a guy. Put her on."

I took the phone upstairs to Kathy and told her she'd have her tea directly. The call had ended by the time I'd returned.

"What did she have to say?"

"Oh, just girl chat. She wondered if I'd seen or heard anything about Ms. Ivey down at the hospice center. She's feeling guilty for not having visited the woman."

We'd rescued Lottie May Ivey from an abusive nursing home a few years back and Queenie had helped nurse her back to health. Two months ago the woman began a rapid decline. Kathy went to see her a couple of times a week. I'd made half a dozen visits.

I took the phone back to the kitchen, warmed my coffee in the microwave, and went back out to the deck. Almost the minute I sat down, the phone rang again. Once again I discussed with myself the merits of letting it go to voice mail. Responsibility won out over sloth.

"Peters and—"

"Yeah. I know who you are, Counselor," the deep, blunt voice announced. "Seen the paper?"

"Yes, Counselor, and I've already talked to Queenie. We were wonderin' if you've been asleep at the wheel, letting the paper spread the news before you did."

"Sad state of affairs, Rick. There are people over at the courthouse these days who don't have the level of respect for a man in my position that they ought. Not sure what to make of it. Maybe my time's over, time to hang up the cleats."

"Or, in your case, the wingtips."

"Yeah. Been a long time since I've been on a ball field. You know what the best part of playing football was? Besides being able to pound the shit out of a bunch of racist white guys? When the game was over, it was over and it was clear who won.

This lawyering game, even if you win, it's not over. There are the appeals, the retrials, the mistrials. Not that all that's a bad thing, mind you. But it lacks a certain, ummm...?"

"Closure?"

"You're a smart man, you know that, Ryder? Anyway, Queenie was not as happy as I expected her to be when I told her the news about her guest's death."

"That must have been right before you called me."

"Indeed. She's afraid the wheels of justice will screech to a halt with this news. When I said I understood her position on the matter but that there was no case to defend her against she really got her hackles up. I wouldn't be surprised if she gets back to you and asks you to stay on the case."

"Exactly what she did a few minutes ago. She's like a dog with a bone, isn't she. She gets it in her head that something's the right thing to do and she's not gonna let go 'til it's done."

"You've got that right, brother. But as far as this office is concerned, the file on the case of Professor Revis is closed."

"I thought you never opened a file on it."

"You know what I mean. And if you wind up workin' for her, try to keep her out of trouble, will you?"

"No mean assignment, I'm afraid."

***

Kathy came out of the bathroom with one towel around her, drying her hair with another.

"You're cute," I said.

"Don't start up with that stuff, Richard. I have work to do this morning."

"Well, so do I. But a little... "

"I'll take a rain check, though."

I groaned, an exaggerated, theatrical sigh.

"You can handle it, Rick. I'm sure you can. Now, moving right along, Queenie mentioned to me that she told you she wants us to work on the professor's murder. Pay us standard rates. A regular gig."

"Well, that's all fine. But first of all, we don't know it was a murder."

"She knows that. And if our investigation confirms it was a suicide, she'll accept that."

"So she says."

"She also said she knows that she can be a little curmudgeonly at times but she thought we all did well together on the Lottie May caper."

Extricating Lottie May from the nursing home where we thought staff, in cahoots with the family, was actively trying to bring about the old lady's demise, was a most rewarding piece of chicanery and great fun. Although it did involve me including shooting a hole in my living room wall, something Kathy was wont to bring up from time to time when she thought I was involved in something that could get out of hand.

When I called to confirm with Queenie what she had in mind, she said straight away, "Yes. I want you to find out what really happened."

"Will you be willing to accept that it was suicide if that's the conclusion Kathy and I come to?"

"Just do the work. Like I told Kathy, I'll pay you your standard rates. If you do your job and you agree that Dr. Revis killed himself, I'll accept it. Won't like it, but I'll accept it. But you'll have to be able to explain to me how you came to that conclusion."

"What if we simply can't find any other conclusion?"

"Just go to work."

"Yes, Ma'am."

"I love ya', Ryder. Tell Kathy I love her, too."

I told Kathy that Queenie loved her and that Audrey and I were going for a walk to look for the perpetrator of Marcellus Revis' death.

"I thought it was a suicide," she said.

"Whichever. The hound and I are going up the road to find out."

"I'll probably be gone by the time you get back. I need to get on the tail of Ms. Marotti. I hate to spend the whole day in the car. But at least I can research potential internet dates while I'm sitting and waiting."

I didn't have to explain to my wife that I wasn't actually going to solve the case by taking a walk with the dog. What I did hope for was some clarity, perhaps even an "ah-ha!" moment wherein pieces of the puzzle would fit together. I would clear my mind and let unexpected connections reveal themselves. After a quarter of a mile or so, none the wiser, we turned around.

Back on the deck with a fresh cup of coffee, it occurred to me that the organizer of the marijuana conference might be able to shed some light on the professor, know something that wasn't available on the computer. I called the Sunset View Resort and spoke to the marketing director who in turn directed me to the office of Dr. Randall Philips at the University of North Carolina at Chapel Hill. Before calling, I looked him up on the university's website.

Philips was a professor in the Pharmacology Department

who was doing research in ethnopharmocology, "the study of ethnic groups and their use of plants as medicine," according to Wikipedia. An ethnopharmacologist seemed like a good fit for someone putting together a conference on the medicinal uses of marijuana and, as I recalled, an area in which Professor Revis also had a PhD.

Voicemail answered. I told it who I was and that I had been retained to look into the circumstances of Dr. Revis's death and could he please call me back. I left a similar message on his email. I expected it would be at hours if not days before I got a reply, if I ever did.

My phone rang five minutes later.

"Mr. Ryder, this is Randy Philips. You just left a message about Marc Revis."

I scrambled to put my thoughts together.

"Thanks for calling back so quickly, Dr. Philips."

"Randy, please."

"Randy, I'm a private investigator looking into the circumstances of Dr. Revis's death. I thought perhaps you'd have some perspective on or information about Dr. Revis that might be helpful."

The pause that followed was long enough for me to think the call may have been dropped.

"You still there, Randy?"

"Are you in Asheville, Mr. Ryder?"

I told him I was.

"So am I. In the general area, anyway. We have a house outside Brevard where we're taking a few days' vacation. Maybe we can get together."

Perhaps Queenie was not alone in questioning the conclusion of the authorities.

We agreed to meet for lunch at a brewery midway between

our locations. It was one of the big-name craft brewers, a recent addition to the area's beer scene. Although not in Asheville proper, it helped substantiate the city's reputation as "Beer City, USA," a step up from an earlier distinction as a good place for tuberculosis treatment.

Philips had told me what he looked like, and there was no mistaking him when he walked into the tap room. An inch or two above my own five-nine, somewhat past middle-age with a full head of disheveled white hair, he looked every bit the college professor in an embroidered pink guayabera shirt over chinos, shod in Birkenstocks and off-white wool socks. I guessed he was ten pounds overweight.

After some introductory chit chat while waiting for our food, Randy said, "You wanted to talk about Marc."

"You're the second person who, after I mentioned something about him, said they wanted to talk to me in person."

"Oh? Who else?"

"Queenie Weaver."

His brow tightened as he tilted his head. "Oh, Queenie ... yes. The woman whose guest house he was staying in."

"She and I go back a few years," I said, "and, although we talked about Dr. Revis the day he was found dead, I discovered that she'd known him better than she'd originally let on."

"At least you and I start on a blank slate with each other," Philips said.

We stopped talking when our food arrived. After tasting it and concurring that it was good, we continued talking between bites.

"Marc Revis was an extraordinarily gifted man. I admired him. I suppose you could say that I envied him. My field is ethnopharmocology. My career has been spent studying how indigenous peoples use plants as medicine. The people who give grants to this kind of work do so not wholly out of their interest in science."

"They want to see a return for their dollar."

"Yes."

"Like studying the specific treatment possibilities of marijuana and getting them patented?" I suggested.

"Exactly like that. Marc was extremely successful in getting funding for his work. Not least of all because of the potential for being almost immediately useful. But also because he was a great salesman. However, it is also true that, although he knew the medical marijuana literature and the potential usefulness of marijuana as medicine as well as anyone, many of his colleagues thought of him as a huckster."

The waitress came and refilled my tea. Philips ordered another beer.

"Two questions arise," I said.

His eyebrows flared. "Only two?"

"Well, for now. One is that 'huckster' implies a degree of dishonesty. Did people think he was dishonest?"

"He was a zealous salesman. Some people thought he was overselling the possibilities of cannabis." His attention wandered when an attractive young woman passed by. When he turned back, he seemed to have lost the thread of the conversation. It was a few seconds passed before he said, "There are there are over four hundred chemicals in marijuana. Only about sixty of them are unique to the cannabis plant—these are the cannabinoids. The most commonly known of these is delta-9-tetrahydrocannabinol, more commonly referred to as THC. It was isolated and synthesized fifty years ago and is the most pharmacologically active and probably the one most responsible for mood-alteration."

"Are you suggesting that there were—are—people who thought that he was overselling the potential for marijuana when there are other plants which have similar properties."

"I see."

I let that stew a minute while I ate. Then asked, "And why would he do that?"

"Because marijuana is sexy right now."

"All right, I get that. But, I'm a detective, Randy, and while this is all very interesting, what has that got to do with Dr. Revis's demise and why you wanted to meet with me."

"How about we finish eating and retire to the patio to continue this?"

After the waitress had left the tabs, Randy said he'd pick them up. I didn't object with the often expected, "Oh, that's okay. I can write it off to my business."

On the patio he ordered another beer. I changed to tonic and lime.

While admiring our surroundings, he took a hefty gulp of brew. "This is hard for me to say. I liked Marc. As I said, he was brilliant. But he was also a con. He came out here not primarily to be the keynote speaker at the conference, although that was important. He came out here to buy land."

If I was still a drinking man, this would be where I would order another. Probably a double of whatever. "What?"

"To buy land."

"How do you know this?"

"He told me."

I said nothing but the question behind my eyes was, He told you?

"Marc trusted me, not in the least because he didn't see me as a threat. Do you have any idea how patronized it feels to know a colleague who is a competitor—in our case for grant money—sees you as 'not a threat'?"

I wrangled that around in my mind.

"Anyway. After the first night of the conference, the night before he was to give the keynote talk, the night before he … died, he smoked some pot. I was surprised, then not surprised if you know what I mean."

"Explain if you would."

"Surprised that this guy who's at the top of his profession engaging in illegal activity with someone he knows as an adversary. But then not surprised because, well, that's how Marc is. Was. I did have some bourbon and he did drink a finger of that."

"That's the second time I've heard that Marc didn't drink but then drank."

"I think when people say that Marc didn't drink, they mean not very much. Certainly not as much as many of his peers. And along with the pot it got his tongue wagging. He told me he had come out here with cash in order to buy land. He said marijuana had been growing in the mountains around here for decades and once it became legal people were going to be stumbling over themselves trying to buy land to grow it. He planned to get in ahead of the rush."

A flood of questions tumbled down on me. Buying up land? How much cash? Where was it? Whose land? Did Queenie know this?

"Let me see if I've got this straight. Marc Revis came out here with the express purpose of buying up land on which marijuana could be grown once it was legalized. And he was the keynote speaker at a conference proselytizing for the legalization of the plant."

"We weren't proselytizing, Rick. It was a scientific

conference to explore the ways marijuana can be used for medical purposes. It's true that a lot of attendees would be pro-legalization or at least pro-medical use. And as for Marc buying land, it wasn't about land on which marijuana could be grown. It was on land on which it will be grown."

"Thanks for the clarification," I said. "I thought most marijuana was being grown indoors these days where you can control the conditions and predict what your product will be like. Outside ... well, you never know."

"That's true. But your overhead is a lot less growing it au naturel. It's very expensive to grow inside. In fact, a lot of indoor growers who learned the trade when it was all underground are going back outside. That was Marc's take on it, anyway. The whole thing about the money may have been BS for all I know. But, he made a big deal of it to me. But also, this is very hush hush. You know... " Philips's voice dropped to a conspiratorial whisper, "'Don't tell anybody.'"

My companion ordered another pint, making it four by my count. I wondered if the establishment would cut him off at some point. I also knew it wouldn't do any good for me to suggest he might be over some limit. I let it go and asked, "How much cash did he have?"

"I don't know. But I sensed it was in the neighborhood of a million dollars."

"A million dollars?" I said it without restraint and realized I'd gotten the attention of some nearby patrons. I returned to my "library voice." "My God. Where was it? I take it he wasn't simply carrying around in a brief case."

"I don't know that either. But he said it was in a safe place."

"This is a million dollars in cash we're talking about?"

"That's what I understood."

"Who else knew this?"

"Supposedly, only me. I guess there were people back in Colorado who knew he'd be looking for land. But supposedly no one knew he planned to buy some on this trip."

"What about the money sources. Wouldn't they know he planned to spend it on this trip? Otherwise, why give it to him?"

"Well, yes. I suppose they'd have known."

Since Queenie had been less than forthcoming about other pertinent details about Dr. Revis's trip, I wondered how much about the land-buying operation was she was familiar with.

"Do the police know that you believe Revis had this kind of cash with him?"

"They never talked to me."

And why would they? I thought. They already had an explanation for his death. They didn't need to know anything else.

"And you don't think that, perhaps, you have an obligation to give them this information. It is very possibly relevant to a murder, wouldn't you say?"

"They've ruled it a suicide."

"Yes, they have. But the fact that he was traveling with this money might be a motive for murder. Heck, maybe you killed him. Maybe you've got the money."

"That's not funny," he said. "In fact, I think maybe this conversation's over, Mr. Ryder."

'This,' came out as a cross between 'thiz' and 'thish.' If I'd been drinking along with him I might not have noticed.

"I'll pick up the extra beers," I said.

"No, no," he said, as he pulled some bills from his wallet and tossed them on table. "Z'on me. I'm the one suggested meeting like this."

We walked out together. When we got to his car, which he found using his keys to make it beep and turn on its lights, I asked if he wanted me to drive him home or call a cab.

"Shit, Rick. My car knows this road. I'll be fine."

I wasn't convinced. Remembering that I'd killed someone while driving drunk, I returned to the restaurant and told the hostess to notify the cops there was a drunk driver on the road. I held my left shoulder toward her so she'd get the point.

Driving home I wondered if I had any responsibility to reveal what he'd told me. It was hearsay, but hearsay only makes a difference at trial. It doesn't take it off the table as something worth investigating. I'd check with my support team; first Kathy, then Nate. I couldn't help thinking about Queenie and what other secrets had she'd been keeping.

I sang along with the old Eric Clapton group, Derek and the Dominos, until my mind went off on a trip of its own. Where it went to was, "a drink of bourbon." With the volume turned down, I remembered what Philips said about himself and Professor Revis having a glass of bourbon along with their pot. It registered at the time, but the money issue was a more immediate concern. Marc Revis, who didn't drink, had at least two glasses of bourbon the night he died. I switched off the music and onto my "Notes" program, to which I dictated, "Revis – at least two drinks of bourbon."

Flat iron steaks were on sale at the local grocery store. In the early stages of our relationship it was obvious that whatever Kathy's talents were—and they were many—cooking was not among them. If I wanted to eat well at home I was going to have to learn how to cook despite my particular physical challenge. Steak, baked potato, and cucumber-tomato salad were not much of a stretch.

The meat was coming to room temperature, a glass of

pinot grigio chilling, as Kathy pulled into the drive. I fixed my tonic and lime, took it and the wine to the back deck, and called Dr. Philips. He'd arrived home safely. I didn't mention the police nor did he. I assumed they hadn't caught up with him. I was okay with that. I'd done what I thought needed to be done.

Kathy knew where to find me. "Fine looking hunk of meat in there," she said after placing a kiss on my cheek and pulling out a chair for herself.

"Good thing you clarified with 'in there.' I might have thought you were paying me a compliment."

"You'd like me to refer to you as 'a fine looking piece of meat'?"

"Been called worse things." I suddenly blushed." "So, how'd the day's sleuthing go?"

"Fruitful. Have I told you about the Marotti's security system that allows them to know remotely when anyone has entered or exited the house?"

"Neat. We ought to get that."

"Why?"

"So I can keep an eye on you. I never know what you're up to."

"Cute, Rick. So, I parked a block away from their house. While I was sitting there, I wondered if we ought to get some of those slap-on commercial signs for the sides of the cars, something that would explain why we might be parked on the street somewhere for a long period of time."

"Probably shouldn't say, 'Peters and Ryder Investigative Services,' huh?"

"Probably not. Although, 'P & R Security Services' might work. Marotti called about eleven and said, 'She's left the building.'"

"Like Elvis."

"Yeah. Of course, he can't tell which way she's going once she's left the house, so I have to put my incredibly intuitive brain to work and decide what to do. She helped me out by passing me from behind before I'd decided on a course of action. Then it was a simple matter of following her."

"Without her knowing it."

"Well, yeah. That's why we get all this money, isn't it?"

"Right. And where'd she go?"

"To that hotel downtown with the public parking garage. I followed her in. She could have been going shopping again. Parking's cheap in those public garages. But she pulled into a 'Hotel Guests Only' spot."

"The plot thickens."

"Indeed, it does. Now I have to decide what to do if she gets on the elevator." She sipped her wine. "I know this is incredibly fascinating. But I'm hungry."

As I fired up the grill, she turned on the oven, put the potatoes in the microwave, and tossed the salad. When the fire was hot, I seared the steaks for a couple of minutes a side, then slid them into the oven to finish. Dinner and refreshed drinks were on the table in twenty minutes.

After we sat down, I said, "My breath is bated. Please, do continue."

"Where were we? Oh, yes. I found a nearby parking spot and followed her to the elevator still wondering, what next. Having learned at the feet of—or, more accurately, in the bed of—the master to simply go with it and see where it leads, I got on and off as she did."

"This is a terrific steak, by the way."

"Glad you like it. On with the story. Did you speak on the elevator?"

"No. We smiled at each other. I followed her down the hall

when she got off. She was letting herself into a room when I said, very dramatically, 'Oops' and turned back toward the elevator. As I passed her I put on a sheepish look and said, 'I'm on the wrong floor.'"

"Think she suspected anything?"

Kathy shrugged. "I have no idea. Nor did I have any idea what to do with what I'd found out except to tell our client that his wife was seen entering a room at a downtown hotel. A room to which, by the way, she had her own key card."

"That's good stuff," I said.

"I guess. Although I've still not been able to identify the person she's seeing."

Clouds were gathering in the west. Thunder rumbled in the distant mountains like Harley Davidsons rambling about the sky.

"Think we can get a walk in?" she asked, eying the sky.

We cleared the table and asked Audrey if he wanted to go for a walk. He could have been auditioning for the circus the way he turned circles in the air.

"To bring this to a close for the day, what have you told Marotti?"

"What I just said. I followed her to a hotel room for which she had her own key. I don't know who, if anyone, was inside the room."

"And you didn't hang around to find out."

"Where would I hang around? If she saw me again, she'd be awfully suspicious."

"What did Marotti say?"

"To keep following her. He's intent on finding out who she's seeing."

"The corporate adversary."

"That's what he wants to know."

We walked in silence letting the sounds of impending weather fill the space. Even Audrey, while running around looking for other wildlife, was quiet.

Eventually, Kathy asked about my day. I recounted it.

"Doesn't that change things? I mean, isn't the money a motive for murder?"

"Seems like it."

"Aren't you going to tell the police?"

"I'm thinking that would be the right thing to do."

"Thinking about it? Rick! How can you not?"

"I know. I also know how much they love it when I meddle in their affairs."

"This is not meddling, for heaven's sake. I actually believe, if I remember my P.I. training correctly, that we are obligated to turn over this kind of information to law enforcement. God! Sometimes I think you really are a prima donna. You're the one who's going to solve the crime. You are the good guy."

"Okay, okay. Got it. Yes, I will call the sheriff's department in the morning."

Four

Thursday

As is generally the case in matters like these, Kathy was right. I did have a vision that I would discover whodunit. I would be the hero. Although, in my defense, that wasn't the only reason I hadn't already passed onto the sheriff what I'd learned. I knew it would mean another visit by them to see Queenie, an encounter I knew would incite another round of outrage.

Kathy was in the office immersed in an internet dating background check. I called the Sheriff's Department, was told that the person I wanted to speak with was Detective Winston Fair, and was put through to him.

"Fair," the voice said. A neutral voice. With no hint of being bothered by the interruption, he told me he would be happy to meet with me and that, unless something unanticipated arose requiring his immediate attention, he planned to be right where he was for the rest of the day.

I hadn't met Detective Fair, but knew him by reputation. He was African American, itself an anomaly in the investigative division of the sheriff's department. He dressed in suits, khaki or gray, white shirts, a necktie, and hand-tooled, made-to-order cowboy boots. When outside, he wore an off-white Stetson hat, also, it was rumored, made to order. The latter two accessories gave rise to him being referred to around the department as 'Cowboy.'

When I arrived at his office, he stood and reached an arm across the desk to take mine.

"Winston Fair," he said.

"Rick Ryder," I replied. "I'm a private in ... "

"Yes, Ryder. I'm familiar with who you are. The arm gives it away. Or rather the lack of one. How'd you lose it?"

"Car wreck. Drunk. Sordid story."

The detective shrugged. "We've all got our share of those. Mine usually involved hitting people. Never ended well."

"You're the guy who pulled a gun on the sheriff, aren't you?"

He raised his hand as if to wave the issue away. "Overmuch is made of it. The gun wasn't loaded. I was turning it in along with my badge."

"Yet, here you are."

"Here I am. And the now-former sheriff is in prison. Enough of that. What can I help you with today, Ryder?"

"Actually, it's more how I might help you."

He leaned back in his chair, a tight, bemused smile forming on his lips. "I'll bite. How might you help me today?"

"It's about the Professor Revis case."

"AKA 'The Pot Professor.'"

"Yes. I know you don't like us private guys messing around in your investigations and this may all be moot if you continue to view Dr. Revis's demise as a suicide. With that in mind, there are a couple of things you might find interesting. The first is not a huge deal, but it is something. Are you aware that Ms. Weaver heard a vehicle pass her house about a half an hour before Revis stopped at her place the night before the body was found? And that her neighbor, Arlo Pressley, saw a vehicle pass his house about ten, ten-thirty that night."

"Nope. Hadn't heard that."

I waited for a few seconds. To end the awkward silence I added, "That suggests someone else was in the area about the time Dr. Revis would have gotten to the cabin."

"And this 'someone else' might have also stopped at the cabin," Fair said.

"It's possible."

"Don't suppose you have any ideas about who this maybe-visitor was."

"No, I don't."

"Okay. You said you had a couple of things. What's number two?"

"According to Dr. Randall Philips, the organizer of the conference where Revis was to speak, Revis had brought with him a significant amount of cash. I understand that you may be aware of that and may, in fact, have the money if there really is any. But if you don't, it might make you look at Dr. Revis' death in a different light. And, by the way, Philips also said that he hadn't been interviewed by anyone in law enforcement."

Fair ignored the last comment and said, "This Dr. Philips thinks that, rather than suicide, Revis was killed for the money?"

"He never said that. It could, however, provide a motive for murder."

He nodded slightly for a couple of seconds, maintaining his neutral expression, then said, "I don't believe you've explained your interest in this matter."

I kept my frustration under control and gathered my thoughts in a way that I could deliver them without making accusations.

"Ms. Weaver is not convinced that Dr. Revis' death is a suicide. She contends that Revis was at a high point in his life, near the zenith of his career, and she can't imagine any circumstances that would have lead him to do that." I thought about adding that she and Revis went back more than forty years and she didn't think it was right that the cause of his death wasn't more fully investigated. But that would pull her even more tightly into the case.

"Did she know about the money?"

"I haven't spoken to her about it."

"Why not?"

The reason I hadn't talked to Queenie about the money was because of her lack of candor with me up to that point. I wasn't sure I could trust her and I didn't want to tell this to the detective since I was still trying to protect her.

"You may understand," I said. "Queenie is not entirely trusting of the Sheriff's Department. She got a very bad taste in her mouth after she was arrested following the murder of that young man on her property. In the current case, she is not dissuaded from her belief that foul play was afoot and she wants us – my wife and myself – to investigate. This visit has two purposes. One, to pass on information that might be relevant to the case. And, two, to find out if your case is closed. Because, if it is, it makes it easier for us to go poking around."

Fair sat in silence, appearing to put his thoughts together. "I'm only telling you this out of professional courtesy, Rick. The case is still open but we're not actively investigating it. If something comes up that leads us to believe the death might have been other than self-inflicted, we'll look at it again."

"Does the information that I just gave you qualify as 'something that has come up'?"

The detective closed his eyes. His face tightened as if someone were turning an invisible vise on his head. When he looked at me again he said, "I know you're a smart man,

Rick. I'm sure you know how departments like this work. The decision whether or not to pursue an investigation is made at levels above me. I do not always agree with them but I have learned to pick my battles. It may not surprise you that the death of a man who came to this area to promote the legalization of marijuana, regardless of the man's credentials, does not instill a great deal of concern in the hearts of many around here. In fact, there are some who think, whatever the cause of death, good riddance."

"So, that's it?"

"Have time to take a walk with me?"

"How long are you talking about?"

"Five-ten minutes."

He donned the hat for which he was so well known. Once outside the building we headed toward the main square of town. Fair took out a pack of Marlboros, smacked one loose and offered it to me. I declined.

"I know. This is a nasty habit. I smoke about one a day. Sometimes none. Sometimes I'm so distraught about something, I'll smoke two."

"That is so unfair," I said. "It's how my wife is. Has one a day. It drives me nuts. I'd like to be able to smoke like that but if I have one, within a week I'll be back up to two, three packs a day."

"Sounds like an addict," Fair said.

"You've got that right."

"You may already have heard that the toxicology report shows Dr. Revis had elevated levels of alcohol and the drug Zolpidem in his system, sufficient to cause respiratory collapse. Zolpidem is the generic name for drugs like Ambien, a bottle of which was found at the scene. The overdose may have been unintentional. Nonetheless, it appears that death was self-inflicted."

I was curious as to how he came to think that I might have know about the tox report, but let it pass and asked, "How do you explain him being found in the outbuilding?"

"You don't die instantaneously when you overdose like that. He could have been disoriented, couldn't remember where he was, went wandering around until he collapsed. I don't want to get too high-handed here, Rick, but we did our detective work. We looked for prints and other evidence about who else might have been at that house that night. We do have a certain amount of professionalism in the department."

"I understand that, Detective. I apologize if I seem to have suggested otherwise. I also understand that you personally are in large part responsible for that professionalism."

"Yeah, I hear that, too. And it doesn't ingratiate me to my peers. There's this idea out there that, in order for a black man to make detective in the department, he must be some kind of genius. I've been doing this kind of work for a long time, first as a Marine MP, then with the Durham police department. I'm well qualified to do this job. I'm no genius. I just do the work."

"And you dress nice," I said with a broad smile, hoping to make it clear I wasn't being sarcastic.

"Yes, there's that, too," he agreed, earning me a slim grin in return.

"You ever get accused that you're copying a character in an Elmore Leonard novel."

"Yeah. I get that some. But there are actually very few people I come in contact with who've ever heard of either the character or the writer. Mostly they think I'm being uppity. Dressing above my rank, as it were. Not just rank in the department, but rank in society. I dress like this because my Mama thought I should always look nice, like I had some class. It wasn't easy raising a black kid in this county back then. Still isn't. When I was in Durham, I found that dressing like this got me a certain kind of respect. So, 'Cowboy' it is."

By now we'd turned around and were approaching his office. At the doors to the building he said, "And now, Rick, as much as I've enjoyed our conversation, I'm gonna have to get on with my work. I appreciate you coming in. I'll make sure that what you told me today will be taken into consideration as we move toward a final resolution of this. If you uncover anything else you think might be reason to take another look at it, let me know. I really do believe in the idea that the bad guys ought to be caught, not in simply closing cases."

We shook hands. I thanked him for his time, not sure my visit had made a difference other than allowing me to get to know the man. Seemed like a nice guy. I did wonder why a man with his experience and background would choose to work in this largely rural county in Western North Carolina.

Back at the car, I realized that I hadn't fully clarified the issue of whether or not it would be considered tampering or interfering if Peters and Ryder actively undertook our own investigation. His parting comment about letting him know if we uncovered anything seemed like tacit approval for our independent investigation.

***

When Kathy returned from snooping into the extramarital life of Wendy Marotti, I called for a staff meeting of the partners of Peters and Ryder Private Detective Agency. Audrey attended ex-officio. Before we got to the formal agenda, i.e., The Investigation into The Untimely Death of Dr. Marcus Arthur Revis, PhD, MD, etc., Kathy wanted to know about my visit to the Sheriff's Department.

"I think Fair will be straight with us if we're straight with him. His name seems apt."

"Think he'll look out for Queenie?"

"What do you mean?"

She shrugged. "I don't know. Another murder on her property. This Detective Fair might be a nice guy but we know there are some in that office who wouldn't be upset if she got her tit caught in the wringer."

"Why, Kathy Peters! I'm shocked. Just shocked."

"Yeah, yeah. You know what I mean."

"Fair knows we're working for her," I said. "I think he'll let us know if anything comes up that might incriminate her."

"But he's not on our side."

"He's on the side of truth and justice," I said.

"You say that with a straight face."

Kathy stood at a white board set on an easel, writing as we came up with ideas about whom we might like to investigate, or investigate further. It was a daunting list.

Kathy said, "This could take forever. Too bad we can't afford an intern."

"Boy, that would be nice, wouldn't it?"

"Maybe Queenie would pop for one."

"I got the impression when I first worked with Queenie that she has a lot of money, inherited from the sale of land by previous generations. I think it's why she's so committed to saving what she has left and as much of it around her as possible. But I'm not sure we could talk her into adding staff to the project."

"But it might actually save her money in the long run. I mean, it's going to take 'X' hours to do the work. Our rates are higher than what we'd charge for a student helping with the work."

"True enough. But where would we put another person?

And we'd have to find someone who knew something about the kind of work we do—maybe someone majoring in Criminal Justice. And even then it would take a lot of orientation."

"You're right, of course. Maybe it's something to look into in the future."

"Maybe. But right now, we've got a lot of work to do by ourselves."

We agreed that I'd start with Dr. Revis's ex-wife and son and Kathy would begin with the hotel staff. Audrey had nothing to offer, having slept through the proceedings.

After adjourning, I went downstairs, accompanied by the Silent Partner. Whenever Kathy or I headed in that direction he assumed it was an opportunity to go outside. Despite the high proportion of disappointments, he always displayed the same intense level of optimism. And in this particular instance, his behavior was reinforced.

Heading up the road away from the house, Audrey took after real or imagined quarry. Since he never captured anything, we never knew if there'd really been something out there or not. Unlike the cats.

While thinking about the best way to get hold of the son and ex-wife and how I would approach them when I found them, I was struck by the idea of going back out to Weaver Mountain and checking the professor's car. It was an almost physical sensation, one of those things that, when it happens to you, you know you're going to have to follow through with it.

Back at the house, the internet provided pictures of the 1991 Jaguar XJS, inside and out. Revis's car had been in cherry condition, even considering it had recently made a cross-country trip. I wondered why it hadn't been impounded.

Kathy came up from the kitchen with fresh coffee for us and saw the monitor as she put my mug down.

"What's that?" she asked.

"The late Professor Revis's car. Not his own, but the type."

"I recognize it. Why are you looking at that?"

I told her of the epiphany I'd had and that I'd be going out to look at it again.

"Why?"

"Let's say, for the sake of discussion, that the Professor did have a lot of cash. If you were traveling cross-country with a lot of cash, where would you stash it?"

"In a suitcase?"

"Possibly. But what if you were worried that you might be stopped for some reason such as having Colorado plates. And you wanted to be sure the money wouldn't be discovered in a routine search."

"You'd do what drug traffickers do and hide it somewhere in the innards of the car."

"Bingo! I thought I'd look for signs that the car had been messed with in anyway."

"And you'd know this how?"

"By looking at these pictures and having an idea what the car should look like and seeing if I noticed any anomalies."

"Anomalies. Good word, Rick. But, like what?"

"I don't know. Won't know till I see it. Maybe a seat doesn't look right. Or one of the interior panels seems like it doesn't fit like it should. You know, sleuth work."

She sat down at her desk facing me. "I don't recall this coming up in the recent discussion, one of what you, in your self-consciously amusing way, refer to as our staff meetings. If I hadn't happened to look over your shoulder would you have let me in on what you were working on? Or would you, as you are wont to do, say something like, 'Going out to Queenie's, see you later,' and be gone leaving me to wonder what you're up to? I think sometimes you forget that I'm your partner here, Rick."

My long years of behaving in ways that were indefensible had taught me to shrink from judgment. I knew I was wrong. What was there to say?

"Sorry. I am sorry. And I could make up an excuse. You know I'm good at that. Instead, I'll continue to work on my thoughtlessness when it comes to our working relationship."

"Thank you," she said. She was mollified for the moment but I knew she was skeptical about how well I'd do the work.

I went the back way up Weaver Mountain to avoid Queenie. The sun glinted off the old Ford truck in the Pressleys' yard as I came around a bend. I closed my eyes against the glare and felt my front tire hit the shoulder. Another second and I would have gone on over the side, down toward the creek. After righting myself, I slowed to see if SaraJean was outside. If she had been, I would have stopped. As it was, I went on up the hill. Where the road splits and the left branch goes off to Tennessee, it passes the spot where marijuana had been found, the pot that landed Queenie in trouble a few years ago. It reminded me of what Dr. Philips said about this being good pot-growing country.

The Jaguar was gone. I could see from fifty yards away that it was not parked in front of the cabin. The universe works in mysterious ways, and I wondered if my inclination to come up here hadn't been somehow ordained. At AA meetings they talk about a Higher Power. I'm a skeptic. But I did marvel that I'd had the thought to come up here. I was going to have to go see Queenie after all.

As always, Sonny escorted me the last several yards to her

house. The ruckus brought her out to the porch.

"Ryder," she said as I stepped out of the car. "What brings you up here? Found the culprit?"

"Afraid not, Queenie. Simple curiosity. I got a bee in my bonnet this morning to come up and take another look at Dr. Revis's car. Imagine my surprise to find it gone."

"Yeah," she said. "His son came down to get it."

"His son?"

"He had to identify the body, you know? A friend had driven him from Blacksburg and brought him up here."

"Ms. Weaver," I said, sitting on my anger. "You have contracted with my wife and myself to help solve the mystery of how Professor Revis died. When conducting an investigation, the more information one has the better. Why didn't you tell us he'd been here?"

"I didn't think it had anything to do with Marc's death. I mean—"

"Queenie! Did you know that Marc had brought money with him, cash supposedly, with which to buy land? That money was hidden somewhere. I think the money could well have been—could still be for that matter—in the car."

"In the car?"

"Yes. In the car."

"I don't think his son knows anything about that."

"How the devil would you know what he was thinking? And, it doesn't matter whether he knows about it or not. Do the sheriff's people know he took the car?"

"I didn't tell them."

"My God. I still don't understand why it wasn't impounded."

"Maybe they didn't know it was Marc's."

"Oh, come on. It was parked outside the cabin where he was staying. All they'd have to do would be to look for the registration."

"Maybe it wasn't there."

I wanted to reach over, put my fingers around her neck, shake her and yell, "Queenie!" It wouldn't have gotten me anything except an outlet for my frustration. What she was saying was true. I told myself to get a grip. I breathed. And breathed again. Said nothing for a minute, maybe two.

"Okay. What's his name and when did he come get the car?"

"His given name in Marcus Arthur Revis, Jr, but he goes by Art. He came by yesterday. I didn't think anything about it till he showed up. Didn't know it would concern you."

"Tell you what, Queenie. From now on, anything—anything!—that happens to you or you hear about that has any connection to Marc Revis, I'd like to know. That is, if you want us to continue with this investigation, of course."

"Come on down off that high horse, Ryder. The altitude's bad for your heart. Want to come up on the porch, have a glass of tea?"

God, she was frustrating.

"You think there's a stash of cash—has a nice ring, don't you think? Stash of cash?—in the car?" she asked after she served our drinks.

"The notion has occurred to me, yes."

"I don't want to do your business for you, but do you think whoever was driving the vehicle that went by here the night the Professor's died might've taken it? If, in fact, there really is a lot of cash."

"That's occurred to me, too. Was my first thought, actually."

"So what got you thinkin' about the car all of a sudden?"

"Don't know. Like I said, I got the notion that I ought to come up and look at the car."

"Been watching too much TV, like that OCD detective who's got special intuition."

We drank our tea, looked out over the southern end of the Blue Ridge Mountains where they flow into the Great Smokies.

"I don't suppose you have a phone number or address for Art Revis, do you?"

"No. But he teaches up at Blacksburg. Shouldn't be hard to find him."

"Virginia Tech?"

"Any other colleges up there?"

"No need to be all snarky. For your information there are a bunch of colleges up there."

"Sorry, Rick. This hasn't been the most fun-filled episode in my life, ya know?"

***

Queenie was right about finding Marcus Arthur Revis, Jr. On the university's website, there was a picture of him along with the phone number of his office. I called, got a recording, and left a message saying who I was, that I was investigating the circumstances of his father's death, and asking him to call back. I thought it a 50-50 proposition I'd hear from him.

My consciousness having been raised, I called Kathy to let her in on my thinking.

"You going to Virginia?"

"Seems like the thing to do. You gotten anywhere yet?"

"The marketing director told me what she'd told you—to contact Dr. Philips. I asked her if there were other staff who were directly involved in running the event. That would be the events director, Janice Bigsby. Very nice woman, good sense of humor. She dealt mostly with Dr. Philips but did remember Dr. Revis very well. Although she only talked with him on the phone, she thought he was very full of himself. Expected special treatment, like the brand of water he would have at the podium, little things like that, even to how high the riser behind the podium should be. She also thought it strange that he wasn't staying at the hotel. The room would have been comped. I told her that he knew the woman in whose cabin he was staying. She still thought it unusual. She also admitted to being relieved when it turned out he wouldn't be giving his talk. Unfortunate, of course, that he was killed. She was very funny about that, knowing how terrible that must sound."

"The picture of this guy gets clearer. Allegedly plagiarizing academic work, maybe some unsavory practices in his research, a demanding prima donna."

"I'm seeing that," Kathy said.

"Ms. Bigsby also said she didn't think there were other staff who had interactions with him since the only time he actually showed up at the hotel before he was killed was at the reception the night before. Hmm. Isn't that interesting? I said, 'killed,' rather than 'died.' Apparently I'm assuming it wasn't suicide."

"Yeah. I'm guilty of that, too. I think we have to be careful we aren't looking for evidence to prove that and not being open to other possibilities."

"Thank you for your insights, Professor Ryder."

"You're welcome. Anything I can do to enlighten the—"

"Shut up," she said.

"Okay. So, what's your next move?"

"I don't know. Probably one of us needs to go to Colorado. And since you're going to Virginia, I guess that would be me."

I didn't say anything.

"Rick? You there?"

In the days when Kathy was traveling with her own company,

we'd had some problems. They weren't fond memories.

"Oh, you know. Old stuff."

"You're gonna have to give that up sometime."

"I'm working on it. I'll go to a lot of meetings while you're gone."

"I haven't really decided if I'll go. Who knows, I may be able to find a lot on the phone and with the computer."

"We both know you get more if you can eyeball someone."

"We'll see. on't go getting your knickers in a twist just yet."

I packed for overnight and called our neighbor. He said that he'd be glad to check on the house if Kathy also left town. His daughter always liked the opportunity to care for Audrey and the cats. Out on the deck, I sat long enough for the whole tribe to come around. Audrey, of course, was there immediately, knowing something was up. The cats, being cats, were more blasé in their arrival. I announced that I'd be gone for a day or two and that Kathy might also be gone and the girl next door would look after them. Even the hound seemed indifferent.

The drive to Virginia would take three-and-a-half hours, give or take. I knew that my quarry might not be there, but the element of surprise was worth a lot. If for some reason the young professor wasn't there I could interview his associates, get an idea of what kind of a guy he was.

I also had time to think about the picture we were drawing of Dr. Revis, Sr. The semi-couth, self-aggrandizing prima donna. This was not the same as Queenie painted him. A committed academic, she thought, not out for personal gain. I wondered if the two pictures could somehow overlap—or if one was buried in the other.

I tossed a small bag with a day's worth of clothes in the back, laid my laptop on the passenger seat and was off for Southwest Virginia. I'd looked the town up on the internet and found that, in spite of the Virginia Tech shootings that occurred in 2007, in 2011 Business Week called it one of the "Best Places in the U.S. to Raise Kids" and readers of Southern Living named it the "Best College Town in the South." I was looking forward to checking this place out as well as advancing our investigation.

At Wytheville, VA, where I-81 meets I-77, about an hour's worth of driving still ahead of me, I questioned the wisdom of making this trip. My butt was sore, my attention wandered, and I had to pee. As I pulled into the exit lane for a rest area, my phone rang.

"I believe I've solved the Marotti case," Kathy said, her voice animated as if she'd won the Detective of the Month prize.

"And, 'Hi' to you, too."

"Yes. Hi. I was about to call him to let him know I'd be gone a few days when he phoned to tell me that Wendy had left the house. I asked if he had any idea where she was going. He said that's what he was paying me to know. I said, 'Mr. Marotti. Because you are paying for our services doesn't give you permission to treat either me or my husband with disrespect.' He apologized and said he'd had a rough morning and he really wanted this thing with his wife resolved. I told him I'd do the best I could.

"On a hunch, I went back to the hotel downtown and pulled into a guest parking lot near the elevator on the ground floor. I figured as long as I was in the car nobody was going to say anything. I was checking out East Colorado faculty on my iPad when who should come out of the elevator?"

"The suspense is killing me. But so is my bladder. I've just pulled into a rest stop and I'll need my wits maneuvering around this place. I'll call you back."

Ten minutes later, I was back on the interstate running on cruise control. When we connected, she picked up as if we hadn't had an interruption.

"She came out of the elevator with a man. Aha, I thought. Nice-looking guy. They walked to her car, they hugged and kissed, although I thought the kiss was rather perfunctory. Maybe they didn't want to draw attention to themselves. I twisted myself around to where I could take a selfie with him behind me. It actually came out quite well. I was delighted with myself and fired it off to Marotti. Presumably this was the guy she'd been seeing.

"It seems that the guy is his wife's brother. Marotti can't stand the guy. Thinks he's gay, something Marotti apparently cannot abide. So when he comes to town to visit, his wife doesn't even tell her husband. Just meets him here and there. Of course Marotti's relieved it's not what he thought it was but he's still not convinced his wife isn't seeing somebody else, too. But for now, he's going to pay us for what we've done—"

"What you've done," I corrected her.

"It's all in the business. Anyway, the case is closed for now. If he suspects anything else, he'll call. Said he was pleased with our—"

"Your."

"Whatever. The work. Another feather in our cap. Now I can go off to Colorado with a clear mind."

"Still want to do that?"

"Somebody's got to. You're not the only one who knows how to interview people."

"Yes, I'm aware of that. And I've already prepared the pets for the eventuality."

After checking into a motel close to campus, I left messages at the younger Revis's university number and on a landline listed for M. Revis, taking a chance that there were not more than one of those in the area.

His call came as I was walking around town reconnoitering dining possibilities. He agreed to meet for dinner while doubting he had any information that would be helpful to our investigation. While waiting on the porch of the restaurant he'd recommended, a flashy new Corvette pulled up. The driver was recognizable from pictures I'd seen of his father. Although he didn't have the older man's ponytail, he had inherited the baldness pattern. He appeared to be my age, give or take a year or two, dressed in jeans, a short-sleeved, blue button-down shirt, athletic shoes.

He had no problem identifying me.

"You share your father's fondness for exotic cars," I noted as we exchanged greetings.

"Yes, I do. And I hope that's the only predilection of his that's been passed down."

I let that pass.

"As I told you on the phone, I don't know how I can help," he said after we'd been seated. "I wasn't involved in his work and didn't know the people he worked with. We weren't close."

"I realize that, Dr. Revis."

"Please call me Art."

"Where's the 'Art' from?"

"By the time I was in high school I was tired of people identifying me with my father, so I just started going by 'Art.' It helped avoid confusion."

We both ordered the mountain trout. The menu suggested a pairing with dry Reisling.

"Want to share a split?" he asked.

"I'll stick with ice tea, thanks."

After the waitress had gone, Art asked, "Not a drinking man?"

"Not anymore."

"The arm have anything to do with that?"

"Has everything to do with that."

I liked this man. He struck me as modest, in contrast what we'd been hearing of his father.

"I don't know what you know about my family history, Rick, but my father almost lost a couple of jobs because of his drinking. He was able to give it up after he discovered pot. He's been a proselytizer ever since."

My eyes must have widened.

"Yeah. That's the story. Well, one of them. He's also a womanizer. Academia being academia, he was able to get a pass on that stuff. And, although he got the drinking under control, I don't think he ever saw the other, the 'sexploits' as people call them, as a problem."

This was terrific stuff, more than I'd anticipated, exactly the kind of thing I'd hoped for.

"What do you know about your father coming to North Carolina to buy land in anticipation of legalized marijuana?"

"Ms. Weaver mentioned something about it."

"But you have no particular knowledge of that other than what Queenie told you?"

He shook his head. "My father's always been a wheeler-dealer. He is—was—a very smart man. Way smarter than me. Brilliant. Two PhD's, a medical degree, does cutting-edge research. One of the reasons we didn't bond very well is that he expected me to be another one of him. He is—was—also arrogant, self-absorbed, petulant and had … questionable ethics."

"And along with all that he was conducting, as you called it, cutting-edge research."

"He was. And not to detract from his work, or to suggest that East Colorado State University is not a fine school, but you notice he was not at any of the major research institutions, which is probably why he could get away with being how he was. They loved him out there because he got buckets of money for the school and put them on the map. He was not, however, overly well thought of by his peers."

"I saw that he was accused of plagiarism some time back."

"There was that. But he was also unwilling to let others get the recognition due them for their participation in the work. As I understand it, there were some who thought he'd outlived his usefulness and was living off his past success. The important current work is being done by his colleagues."

"Do you suppose there was enough animosity for someone to want to kill him?"

"I thought it was a suicide."

"Officially, his death was due to an overdose of drugs and alcohol. According to the lead investigator, they're going with the assumption that it was either accidental or intentional. Self-induced either way. However, they haven't closed the case."

"You think someone would make the trip to Asheville and somehow get him to ingest enough alcohol and some kind of drugs—"

"Ambien," I offered. "A sleeping pill."

"How would you do that?"

"I don't know. Put the drug in his bourbon."

"Like a Mickey."

"Exactly. Interestingly, your father, who supposedly didn't drink, had at least two glasses of bourbon and smoked some pot before he got back to the cabin that night. At which point it may not have taken much to talk him into another one—or more."

"Where and how would someone get the pills?"

I shrugged. "This is all speculation of course, but maybe someone knew or assumed he kept them in with his toiletry things and grabbed some on a trip to the john. Maybe someone who knew he was taking the drug brought their own supply."

"That's kind of stretch, isn't it?"

"Like I suggested, it's all kind of a stretch at this point."

We finished our meals and ordered coffees, mine plain, his Irish.

"Changing the topic somewhat, I'd like to ask you about the car."

"The Corvette?"

"No, the Jag."

"Ah, yes. My inheritance."

"Oh?"

"Yes. Literally. My entire inheritance."

"Meaning?"

"That's it. There's nothing else. The man had no money. He lived off the grants he got. Administrative costs. I guess he did some very creative bookkeeping."

"Any chance I can see it? It's pretty special, I understand."

"You know anything about classic cars?"

"No. Only what I looked up about that one."

Unlike Dr. Philips, young Dr. Revis was very happy for me to cover the check. His house was near campus, in an area that appeared to be re-gentrifying, homes I imagined were built as faculty housing, abandoned for the suburbs fifty or sixty years ago and re-discovered in the past couple of decades. His was two stories, white shingled, blue trim, with neat gardens in front and on the sides. Very comfortable without excess. A gray pickup truck sat in the driveway. I wondered if Kathy and I were the only people in America who still didn't own a pickup.

The Jaguar was parked alongside the driveway protected by a fitted cover. Art unveiled the vehicle as if it were an original Rembrandt. I felt I should applaud.

While we were giving the car the once over, I said, "So, where would you stash upwards of million dollars on a trip out here from Colorado, assuming you weren't carrying it in a suitcase?"

The younger Revis scrunched his face. "How many $100 dollar bills would $1,000,000 be? 10,000 bills, right? As I understand it, Colorado is awash in that kind of cash these days, one of the unintended consequences of legalization." His voice had begun to rise. "And when I think about it, the more the idea of suicide seems to be a cover-up. Somebody doesn't want anyone to follow where that trail leads."

His face had reddened, his whole body seemed to have tensed. It wasn't petulance. It wasn't arrogance. He was angry that what seemed to be obvious wasn't being taken that way by the authorities. I thought he was probably right and did my best to maintain my neutral, investigative demeanor.

He took a breath and stretched his neck and shoulders.

"Sorry, Rick, but ..."

"No need," I said.

"Well, I think Ms. Weaver's right. There's something else going on here. Anyway, the car then. I don't know if you know what my academic field is—"

"Materials Science and Engineering."

"Done your homework. That's heartening. After Ms. Weaver told me about the money, I looked this car over for any place I thought it—assuming there really was all that money— could have been stashed. I've given the car a pretty good going over, and its physical integrity is intact. If it was in the car, it's gone now, and whoever did the hiding and removal did an excellent job."

"You mean no body parts or upholstery were altered to make places for the cash."

"Not that I can tell. My father was not one for working with his hands. If the money was hidden somewhere like, say, in a door panel, someone else would have to have done the work. And then someone would have had to reverse the process once he got to his destination."

"Mind if I sit in it?"

He did not. Even without the car in motion, I got a sense of what it might feel like on the road, and why a person would covet it. I scanned the interior and, compared with the photos I'd looked at, nothing seemed amiss. Art went around to the back of the car, and I got out and joined him. When he opened the trunk, we peered inside as if the truth were hidden there, even if the money wasn't.

"We could go sit on the patio with cold drinks rather than stand around waiting for something to happen," he said. "Mind if I have something stronger than tea?"

"Absolutely not."

It was a very southern space. More flowers and a small vegetable garden, in the back yard, the smell of a summer afternoon. On the patio, white wicker furniture and a slowly whirring ceiling fan. I could imagine us on a veranda somewhere in Alabama or Louisiana.

"Who's got the green thumb?" I asked.

"Not me, that's for sure. Mine's black, then came back out with two mint julep glasses, even including sprigs of mint. Mine was tea; his, I presumed, was a julep. He sat down and sipped appreciatively, then looked at me inquiringly.

"I was thinking about scenarios," I told him. "Say someone from East Colorado knows he has this bundle of money and comes from out there to kill Marc. If the money was contained in the car itself, the perpetrator may have concluded that he couldn't dismantle the thing on the property out at Queenie's where's he's likely to be discovered. He'd need to take the car to another location. If that were the case, you'd expect he would have taken the car since a reasonable person would assume that, one way or another, the car wasn't going to be staying there long. Along with your assessment, I think that scenario is unlikely. Another possibility is, although to me it's counter-intuitive, your dad had the money in a suitcase, briefcase, some kind of luggage with him in the cabin. Presumably out of sight. We believe that a car—quite likely a pickup truck—was in the neighborhood of the cabin around the time your father would have gotten back from the hotel that night. That person gets Marc dosed up, lets him wander, or directs him to the outbuilding where he proceeds to pass out. He then has time to search his stuff."

"How long would it take for the alcohol and drugs to take effect?"

"Depends on what he had before he got back to the cabin. As I said, we know he had at least two bourbons and smoked some dope."

Art looked skeptical. "Somehow this mythical person from Colorado is able to get him to ingest enough of the sleeping meds to kill him. And why would it have to be someone from East Colorado?"

"Doesn't have to be. As I said, talking 'what if'."

"While I was in fixing the drinks I was doing some creative thinking as well," he said. "All kinds of people are coming out of the woodwork around this marijuana legalization campaign. Including the kind of people who were supposedly funding my father's trip out here. Some of those are not nice people."

"By 'not nice people' are you thinking individuals or something more insidious like organized crime?"

"Of course, as speculation, it could be either. But I was thinking more of the latter. If some of the right—or wrong, depending on how you look at it—people got a whiff that Marc was driving out here with a million dollars, they'd have no qualms about doing what they had to do to get their hands on that money. And you know they have people who can tear down a car and put it back together in nothing flat."

"Why wait till he gets out here? Why not waylay him on the road?"

"He had a passenger with him, didn't he? You'd have to deal with that person, too. Less complicated to do it while he's alone." He set his drink down and leaned back hard in his chair. "I can't believe the police aren't working on this. A million dollars disappears and they're not looking for it?"

"You need to remember, the money is hearsay. As far as I know, Dr. Philips, the guy who organized the conference, is the only one who's mentioned it. And he didn't actually see it. There's no evidence that the money ever actually existed."

"What about Ms. Weaver?"

"Oh. Yeah. I guess I was thinking about people who might have known about it before he got to North Carolina."

"Dr. Philips knew before Dad arrived in Asheville?"

"He did. He's the one who got your father to be the keynoter at the conference."

"Wouldn't he be a suspect?"

"Oh, yes. He was the first person on our list."

We sat some more. The light was fading. The aroma of rosemary drifted over from a nearby herb garden.

"What if Dad made that story up?" Art asked. "About the money. Something to make him more important and to add a bit of intrigue to things. Not the kind of thing my father was averse to doing."

***

Back in the day when Kathy traveled a lot with her own business, we began a routine in which, if one of us was out of town, the traveler called home at 10:00 p.m. The clock on my motel-room nightstand showed 10:02 when she answered.

After I'd told her of my conversation with Art Revis, she asked the inevitable. "Do you think he did it? Think he's got the money?"

"As for as him 'doing it,' as you so delicately put it—" Another of those thundersriking thoughts struck me. "Oh, my god. He drives a gray pickup truck. I hadn't thought anything about it at the time. That's how good a sleuth I am."

"Rick. Come on. How many people drive gray trucks these days? It seems like every other vehicle on the road is a gray or silver truck. Did you know that pickup trucks are not only the best-selling vehicles but the three best-selling vehicles in the country?"

"That's impressive. Where'd you learn that?"

"I don't know. Heard it on some radio or TV program I guess."

"Art also told me that he didn't drive to Asheville to get the Jag. Supposedly got a ride with a friend who was going to Asheville for a meeting. I assumed that would have been the day after he died, but he could have been at the cabin when Marc got there. He knows about his father's issues with alcohol. It wouldn't be unreasonable to think he knew about the sleeping pills. He could have brought his own supply. I understand it's not hard to get that stuff."

Kathy took it from there. "So he spikes his father's drink. Father passes out. Art has time to look for the money, either in the car or around the cabin."

"Then drags or carries the body into the little barn."

"He kills his own father," she says.

"Maybe he didn't plan to. Was only going to incapacitate him for a while. Misjudged the dosage. When he told me about inheriting the car, I thought he sounded resentful. Maybe this was this way for him to get what he thought was his due."

"That's harsh, don't you think?"

"Yes. But a million dollars, or the possibility of a getting a million dollars, can do strange things to people. And Art and his father weren't what you call best buddies."

"Wow. That's still hard for me to get my head around."

"Toughen up. Sam Spade wouldn't have found it exceptional."

"I think I'm more in the Nora Charles vein. Okay. Moving on. So, who else is on the list?"

"Queenie."

"You're kidding?"

"I'm not. It's a long shot, but she had the opportunity."

"Motive?"

"This guy's going to facilitate the purchase of land which will then be clear cut for the cultivation of marijuana. You know what she was like last time she got involved with people she called land-rapists."

That case involved Lottie May Ivey. Lottie May's land was adjacent to Queenie's, and developers engaged in shady behavior while trying to get the two womens' land, on which they wanted to build a gated golf-course community. That crowd went so far as to burn down the old lady's house to get her out of the way. Queenie had not reacted well.

"I remember," Kathy said. "Who else?"

"Philips. He could have gone out there that night."

"Does he drive a gray truck like everybody else in the world but us?"

"It's not what he was driving the day we met, but that doesn't mean he couldn't own one."

"Motive?"

"Professional jealousy, for one. And a whole lot of money."

"Others on your list?" she prodded.

"The mob."

"The mob?"

"Yeah. As Art pointed out there are all kind of people getting involved in the marijuana business. People who have been in the marijuana business. People in organized crime may like the idea of legalization. It makes it easier for them to know who to go after, who to subvert. If someone of that ilk hears about what Marc is up to, they might not hesitate to come out here, off the guy and take the money."

"I don't know much about organized crime, Rick, but what happened to Marc doesn't strike me as the stereotypical mob hit."

"What would strike you as one?"

"Oh, I don't know. They'd be less concerned about making it look like a suicide."

"I don't know much about how organized crime works except what I see in the movies. It doesn't strike me that way, either. Not out of the realm of possibilities, I suppose."

"Maybe I'll learn more out in Colorado."

"So, you're going."

"You okay with that?"

"Yes." I meant it. Mostly.

Five

Sunday

She called before boarding the plane at seven in the morning on her way to Charlotte, where she would get to cool her heals for three hours before continuing to Denver. We commiserated about the sad state of air travel these days. I thought perhaps she was trying to make me feel not so bad about her going and leaving me behind.

I love to drive. After my catastrophic wreck when I was eighteen, I was afraid I'd never be able to get behind the wheel again. That fear was greater than worrying about how I was going to live with one arm missing. Getting my first custom-designed car was the greatest thrill of my life up until then. I try not to be too cavalier about the responsibilities and opportunities this affords me—although there are times when Kathy has to remind me of what I'd be giving up if I had another serious mishap. So, as long as I'm not being chased or chasing someone, I tend to be very conservative in my driving habits. Driving at a moderate rate as opposed to pushing it as hard as I could without being stopped allows my mind to mull over things other than keeping the car on the road. For instance, what really happened to Dr. Marcus Revis and, if a crime had been committed, who was the culprit?

The drive back to Asheville gave me lots of mulling

time. Occam's razor suggests that the most likely answer to a problem is the simplest. I didn't like it since it seemed as if Queenie fit that bill with opportunity, motive, and method. While I had said to Kathy that she was a long shot, she was the one in closest physical proximity. She knew when he'd be home. They'd drunk bourbon together. It was not unlikely that she knew about his sleeping pill use. If there really was money and she found it, I wouldn't be surprised to hear about an anonymous contribution to a land conservancy or some such outfit in the near future.

As for Philips and Marc's son, Philips didn't seem like the murdering kind, but I knew that was often illusory. Art was the least likely of the bunch but couldn't be ruled out. When I found I wasn't paying close attention to the road, I lectured myself about leaving this alone for the time being. Kathy's investigations in Colorado might shed some light. Until then it was all idle speculation, our favorite game.

When I arrived home at noon, Audrey was beside himself. On top of himself, under himself, around himself. He could not believe that, once again, I'd returned. Oh, how grand! The cats? Who knew where they were? I called my neighbor Eric to let him know I'd returned.

"Couple of guys came by. Said they were doing some work for you. I didn't think they looked like people you'd be working with."

"Oh?"

"I was raking leaves in the front yard yesterday when a car passed. You know that's not a regular occurrence out here. It was a beat-up old pickup. Didn't look made for the terrain in the forest so I walked out on the road to see where it went and saw it in your driveway. I didn't see anybody for a minute until someone came from around the back of the house. I walked over to see what was up and he said he was doing some work for you. Then this other guy came from around the back. I didn't ask what kind of work they were doing although they didn't look much like working kind of men if you know what I mean. Not the kind I'd want my daughter hanging around with. And I thought you would have told me you were expecting someone. They kind of gave off a 'what's it to you' attitude although they didn't say that."

"What did they look like?" I asked, wondering if I knew either of them, although no one I knew was planning on doing any work at the house.

"Couple of good ole boys, dressed in jeans and t-shirts with the sleeves cut off at the shoulder, old beat-up cowboy boots. One had a pony tail; the other's hair hung down to his shoulders. I just stood there until they finally went back to their truck and drove off. Oh, yeah. Here. I have the license plate number."

I scowled. This couldn't be good. "What color was the pickup?" I asked, what with gray pickups seeming to show up here and there.

"Gray."

"Jeez! Does everybody have a gray pickup other than us?"

"I don't."

"You and me. The guys without gray pickups. At any rate, it was nobody doing work for me. Thanks for keeping an eye out for us."

"I'm sure it's nothing to be worried about." But out here at the edge of civilization, we both knew it was.

I was creeped out by the idea of unsavory-looking types wandering around my house when I wasn't home, and I was glad Kathy'd been away. Then I wondered if these guys knew somehow that we were both gone. That was even creepier. I got chills thinking that perhaps Eric had scared them off from breaking in. Or maybe they'd gotten in and were on their way out. Although we had a security system that would have notified us in case of a break-in—and hadn't—I went ahead and inspected the house anyway, from the top floor to the basement and out on the deck. Then I took Audrey with me for a walk-around outside. Although my companion found lots to interest him, nothing suspicious turned up. A phone call to the security company confirmed that they'd not been alerted to any activity.

***

While setting up chairs for the 8:00 p.m. meeting at the Presbyterian Church, I saw my sponsor and told him Kathy was out of town. Jim had helped me through my earlier 'Kathy difficulties' revolving around her travel.

"How're you doing today?"

This was a version of AA's "one day at a time" aphorism.

"The Serenity Prayer and meetings help," I said. "I believe Kathy and I both have accepted that we are flawed people who do stupid things from time to time but that neither one of us is likely to repeat what almost destroyed our marriage."

The speaker for the evening talked about acceptance, always something good for me to hear. Afterwards, I declined the invitation to go for coffee.

Her call came at 10:04. Once the greetings were out of the way, she said, "I've been thinking about Queenie as your number one suspect. Why would she hire us to find out who killed the man if she was the one who did it?"

"Classic misdirection. The person who appears to be most interested in finding out who the guilty party is, is the guilty party herself. You have to admit she's done some questionable things during our investigation, like not bothering to pass on important information. All the more reason to continue on and see how this develops. What have you learned out there?"

"The academic bureaucracy is worse than any government. Well, maybe not Russia, which I understand is pretty Byzantine. It took me most of the day to get hold of someone who'd worked with him."

"That's not too surprising, is it, given it's Sunday?"

"I guess. I finally reached Dr. Stanley Greenfield, former assistant manager of The Institute for the Study of Cannabis and Health. Marc's institute. Dr. Greenfield agreed that Marc was a brilliant man who also played loose with the rules of academic research. According to him, although Revis did have his admirers, there was a growing list of people who didn't like him personally and did not want to work with him, who thought he was self-aggrandizing to the detriment of his colleagues. We've heard some of the other words people have used to describe him, like 'arrogant' and 'abrasive.'"

"Pretty much what Dr. Philips had to say about him."

"Greenfield mentioned two others who had had recent run-ins with him. One was apparently a personal matter; the other was more of a professional nature. I've got appointments with both of them in the morning. Depending on what I learn, I could be home tomorrow night."

"That would be nice."

We had said our 'good-nights' before I remembered my conversation with Eric.

"You know," she said, "after that one time we were broken into, the security company suggested we have some cameras installed outside. You think maybe it's time to do that?"

"I hate it because it reinforces the idea that we're not safe and need to live in fear."

"The idea, I believe, is that by taking these steps, it reduces one's fear."

"I'm not so sure of that. But you may be right. I'll call them in the morning."

I wasn't convinced they'd do much good, but at least it would be doing something and giving us a sense of control over things, however delusional that sense might be.

Six

Monday

When Kathy was away, the only difference in my morning routine was that I didn't take tea to her. I exercised in the basement gym, showered, and breakfasted on the deck with whichever of the menagerie chose to accompany me. On Mondays I ate light, knowing I'd be meeting Nate at the bakery.

Arriving before he did, I got a pastry and coffee and found a booth. Five minutes later one might have imagined the President of the United States had arrived. Very few people who inhabited downtown did not know the big man. The impact of the good cheer showered upon him wore off quickly after he sat down.

"White people," he said, not in an admiring sort of way.

"Well, yes, and good morning to you, Counselor."

"Present company excluded, Counselor."

"Excluded from what?"

"From my generally negative view of people of your ilk."

"My ilk?"

"Oh, don't play ignorant. White people. You know. Them what runs everything."

"Everything in the immediate case being ... ?"

"The ironically named Criminal Justice System."

"This have anything to do, perhaps, with the client you mentioned, the one with the son who got kicked out of school?"

"Has everything to do with it. And in particular, Judge Harold J. Beeson. You know His Honor—and I use that term very lightly."

"Heard of him."

"Next time he's on the ballot you make sure to get all your people to vote against him. The man gave my client thirty days of active time. Because he mouthed off at a couple of school people and an almost rent-a-cop."

"That last would be the school resource officer?"

"Yeah. The kind of cop they won't let out on the street. Gotta hang around the school house, make sure all the kiddies behave."

"Well, my man, seems you got some attitude here."

"I'll say I have some atti-fuckin'-tude. I want to appeal it. Wouldn't be hard to show racial bias against that honky, but it would take research to show his pattern and I don't have that kind of time or resources anymore, bein' semi-retired. Hah! Semi-retired. That's a laugh."

"How's your blood pressure these days, Nate?"

"You sound like my wife. 'Now calm down, Nate.'"

"Might think about it, ya know?"

"I know. I know. Okay, that's life in my part of town. What's happenin' out in the boonies?"

"Hardly the boonies, Nate."

"Got a lot of brothers out your way?"

"No. We don't."

"'Cause it's the boonies."

"Okay, Nate. Out in the boonies we're trying to find out what really happened to Professor Marcus Revis."

"He of the 'let's-legalize-pot' fame."

"Not to mention the 'What-Are-the-Medicinal-Properties-of-Marijuana?' fame."

"Yeah. Man just wants to do good for humanity. Like all those potheads runnin' round naked, bangin' drums out at that Burnin' Man thing."

"Not sure I get the connection, Counselor."

He waved a dismissive hand.

We moved on to less contentious matters, how our respective wives were doing, the vagaries of the weather, until he said, "I guess I should be going. See what I can do about getting my man out of the slammer."

***

The light in my mind clicked on as I walked toward my car. It shone its light on Revis's ex-wife. Ex-spouses in general often have reasons to off their former mates. Perhaps Art could fill me in on the current state of his mother's and father's relationship. I left messages for him at work and home.

We had several open files of internet dating clients in the R & P Agency office. Checking them seemed like a healthy diversion while I waited for Art to get back to me. The cases were all easy, the clients' potential dates appearing to be who and what they said they were based on all sources we'd had contact with. I was happy to tell the clients what I'd found and that the bills would be in the mail.

Lunch was a sandwich and salad on the back deck with Audrey for company. I like having him around, but he doesn't keep up his end of a conversation very well. From up in the bedroom I heard a nap calling. I'd gotten as far the edge of the bed and had my shoes off when the phone rang.

"I know there was a long period when mom and dad had almost no contact unless it concerned me," Revis told me after I explained why I'd called him. "They'd begun communicating again, by phone as far as I knew, or maybe the internet. It seemed strange to me. But I operate on the philosophy that the more people get along the better."

"You have any idea what they might have been in conversation about?"

"No. I assumed that it had been a long time, hurts had healed, and they—well, I assume it was my mother—wanted to get all that negative stuff behind her."

"What kind of negative stuff?"

There was a pause before he said, "You've been finding things out about my father. He was not a particularly nice guy. Emotionally abusive, had serial affairs, and was a real lousy father. As I said, I was surprised when I heard from her that they'd been back in contact."

I didn't know how to put the next question so that it didn't sound like what it was. I decided there was no other way, so I asked. "Do you know if she knew about the money?"

"You're asking if she might have killed him for it?"

"I guess I am."

I waited through the next pause.

"No. I don't. Money or no money, I can't imagine her doing that. I know all the stuff about how you never know what people are capable of. And maybe he just continued to piss her off and she didn't know any other way to cut the ties. But how does that fit with her resuming contact with him?"

"Maybe she wanted to be able to keep tabs on him, keep up with where he was."

"So she could find a convenient place to murder him?" he asked, his tone thick with incredulity.

When I closed my eyes I saw him at his desk struggling with the idea that one of his parents might have killed the other. Even for a grown man, that notion had to be a mind-bender.

Anne Revis, née McDonald, was now firmly on the suspect list.

As if he were clairvoyant, he said, "Here's a number if you want to contact her. She wasn't involved, though."

"A moment ago you didn't sound quite so sure."

"I was ruminating."

***

Five minutes after I'd left a message for her, Anne returned the call.

"Ms. McDonald, thanks for returning my call. My name is Rick Ryder and I'm a detective looking into—"

"Yes, Mr. Ryder. I know who you are. You are investigating the death of my former husband, Marc Revis."

I assumed she'd had a very recent conversation with her son.

"I'm sure you know that the police consider the death as self-inflicted, either accidental or suicidal. But they haven't closed the case, which means they are, presumably, open to other possibilities."

"Including the possibility that he was murdered, you mean."

"Yes, that's what I mean."

"And how is it you think I might be able help you?"

"I have no idea other than providing some background information about your former husband. Your son told me that you and Marc had been back in contact recently."

"Life's short, Mr. Ryder. Holding negative thoughts about

people is bad for one's chi, one's spirit. I thought it was time to get past all the animosity there was between us. I had no interest in renewing any kind of intimate relationship with him, but I did hope we could be civil with each other. After all, we do have Art."

Cynicism is one of the job qualifications for this line of work. It's not the noblest of human attributes and, in spite of it, we continue to be fooled a lot. If I were a cop, the next question would have been, "Where were you on the night before Marc was found dead?" But I'm not a cop, so I asked where she was living now.

"I'm back in Celo."

I imaged she could hear my eyebrows rising.

"You're surprised."

"To be honest, yes. Although I'm not sure why."

"I spent many years here. It's a wonderful place. I saw no reason to let what happened between Marc and myself keep me from enjoying it. It was after I returned here that I decided to reconnect with him. You ought to come up here some time, Mr. Ryder. It's really special."

"I've heard that. I might take you up on it."

"If you do, call me. I'd be happy to show you around."

After we'd said goodbyes, it struck me that she had maneuvered us to the end of the conversation.

In the midst of pondering the pros and cons of making the short trip to Art's hometown, Kathy called. The excitement in her voice reminded me of the days when she owned her own business and would call from the road after making a big sale. After a perfunctory "Hi, Hon," she said, "It seems likely that Dr. Revis did have the kind of money Dr. Philips mentioned. I spoke to a former colleague, Dr. Kenneth Wyans, who's about to leave the university in part because of the favoritism Marc receives."

"I believe you mean, 'received.' I don't think the man's going to be getting any more special treatment."

"Cute."

"He got that treatment because of the grant money he was able to get, right?"

"Yes. And, because of the work his lab is doing, the university is getting a kind of recognition it hadn't had before. According to Wyans, a consortium of people and organizations interested in the legalization of marijuana across the country pooled their money for him to use to buy land on his trip east."

"Why wouldn't these people simply buy the land themselves?"

"No one would be surprised that a guy like Revis would be interested in buying land in the interest of growing marijuana to further his research. On the other hand, these anonymous backers don't want their names publicly associated with marijuana. Also, Marc was going to be out there. You know. Boots on the ground. That seems to confirm that there's upward of a million dollars floating around somewhere. Also, other than his beloved Jaguar, apparently Revis maintained a very modest lifestyle. Wyans acknowledged there was a certain amount of grudging admiration for that and for the fact that he didn't appear to be trying to get rich. He believed in the work he was doing, even if he was a jerk in the way he went about it. Wyans thinks that all the money he took with him would go where it was intended."

"To buy land," I said.

"Wyans thought that some of it was going to be spent on educating politicians about the benefits to the state of it being legalized."

"I guess 'educating' is a nicer word in this context than buying their votes."

"I believe the correct word is—"

"Lobbying," I cut her off. "Yes. A noble pursuit. Such a boon to democracy that so many people want to engage in our political process. And I'm sure the only reason politicians take money from these 'educators' is to—"

"Got your point, dear."

"All right, all right. I don't know if I mentioned this to you, but Detective Fair gave me the idea that there are people in the Sheriff's Department who wouldn't be too upset if somebody like Professor Revis met an untimely fate. Did Wyans think that Revis was an important enough guy in the legalization movement for someone—or, some people—to think he had to be stopped?"

"You think the sheriff's department had something to do with this?" she asked.

"Not actively."

"But maybe passively?" she ventured. "You're suggesting that there could have been collusion between law enforcement and ... whoever might have killed him?"

"It's a possibility. If not before the fact, maybe after the fact."

"Covering it up, you mean?"

"Just thinking out loud."

"You sure get yourself in the middle of stuff, don't you, Mr. Ryder?"

"Hey, you're a party to this, too, Ms. Peters. And when are you coming home?"

"There's another person I want to talk to. She's an assistant of Marc's who's been with him for a long time. Wyans suggested she might have information about some of the people who were underwriting the land acquisition. But I can't talk to her until tomorrow."

"What are going to do the rest of the day?"

"There are some nice hiking trails nearby. It is Colorado, after all."

I flashed on other opportunities she might have with all the healthy young men floating around that part of the country, but I held my tongue. "Enjoy yourself. Stay out of jail. I miss you. You flying out tomorrow?"

"Depends on when I can get a flight."

"Okay. Call me when you know something. I love you."

I waited through a moment of dead air.

"Kathy?"

"There's one other thing."

My body sagged. "Yes?"

"I'm having dinner with Dr. Wyans."

I gave her the dead air back.

"Rick? Are you going to be okay with this?"

"Yes, I'm okay with it. Just the old stuff. It's still there, I'm afraid. Thanks for telling me about it. It feels … clean."

"That was the idea. I didn't want to come home and say, 'Oh, by the way I had dinner with this guy.'"

I was almost okay with it by the time we did say our pro forma 'I love you's. Not our good-nights, though. Those would come later, at 10:00.

I went to a four o'clock meeting. I called Jim. We agreed to grab dinner together before the next one, at eight. I drove out to the Arboretum, walked around, did everything possible to keep the demons at bay.

"Anything up?" my sponsor asked after we were seated at a small Greek-Italian place.

"The usual."

"Kathy out of town?"

"I'm transparent, aren't I? That's a good thing, isn't it?"

He agreed it was.

The phone had not rung by 10:05. Nor at ten after. I told myself to relax. Something innocent had delayed her call. By 10:20, my heart was racing. I told myself to breathe. The only two possible reasons I could think of for her not calling, in addition to merely not paying attention to the time, were equally painful for me to consider. She was with that guy or she'd been in an accident. Or, maybe she'd forgotten about the time zone difference. Audrey sensed something was amiss and huddled close to my feet.

The unknowing was unbearable. I called.

"Hi, hon," I said to voice mail, hoping she wouldn't hear the fear in my voice. "Just wondering where you are. It's eleven o'clock here. I'll be turning in soon but call me as soon as you hear this. I love you."

Adrenalin kicked in and I couldn't sit still. After a couple of trips around the house I got in the car with no idea where I was going. My mind wouldn't let go of unthinkable circumstances that might account for her not calling. I wound up at the supermarket out on the highway, thinking cold and sweet, ice cream, or maybe fatty and salty, like macaroni and cheese. After aimlessly wandering, I found myself at the checkout line with a pint of pistachio ice cream and a six pack of beer. People not familiar with addiction might wonder how a man who had lost an arm and almost lost the love of his life to alcohol could even consider taking a drink. The truth is, I hadn't considered it. It was not a conscious decision. It was if I'd been in a blackout.

Sitting in the car, my hand shaking as if palsied, I took one of the beers out of the pack, stood it between my legs, and removed a Swiss Army-type knife with bottle opener from the glove box. I sat for what could have been two minutes or twenty minutes with the opener poised on the beer bottle. I vaguely heard a knocking sound followed a few seconds by a louder knock. I lowered the window. In the otherworldly glow of the parking lot lights I could tell he was an older man wearing a white shirt. I recognized him as one of the store managers.

"Excuse me, sir. Are you okay?"

"Boy, that's a good question," I said.

"One of the boys came in and said he saw you slumped over. He was worried something might have happened to you."

"It's good you have attentive employees. I'm fine. Really. Just had a hard day. But will you do me a favor?"

"What's that?"

I put the bottle I had in my hand back in its carrier and lifted it across my body. "Take this. If you don't, I'm going to have to leave it in your parking lot."

"Did you buy that here?"

"Yes, I did. And changed my mind about drinking it."

"You want a refund?"

"No. Just get it away from me."

He took it, said, "Be careful, bud," and turned away.

Heading back out Riceville Road, struggling to see past the mist in my eyes, I caught the flashing blue lights in the rearview mirror. I pulled into the community center a quarter mile or so down the road and turned my flashers on. I had the window open when the cop walked up to me.

"Good evening, sir."

"Evening, Officer," I said, I handing him my license and registration. He took them back to the cruiser. When he returned, he said, "You're that private detective lives out here, aren't you?"

I agreed I was.

"Have you been drinking tonight, Mr. Ryder?"

"No, sir."

"Would you might stepping out of the car, sir?"

I obeyed. He had me do the finger to the nose thing and to walk ten feet away from him and return. "Thank you, sir. The manager of the Superfoods store you just left called. He wasn't sure you'd been drinking but was worried because of the way he found you in his parking lot. You're not far from home are you?"

"No, sir."

He handed back my papers. "Drive safely and have a nice morning."

The phone call I made to her when I got home met the same response as my earlier one. I had no idea how to make it through the night. I thought again of Jim.

"I hate to wake you at this hour," I said.

"That's what sponsors are for," he assured me.

"Kathy's not returning my calls."

"That's gotta be tough," he said.

Laughter spilled out of my mouth. That was Jim. The man did not let you get away with drama. He was not unkind or uncaring. Exactly the opposite. He meant it when he said it's got to be tough. And he was fine being wakened at three a.m. to hear a hurting soul. And that's exactly what he would do. Hear. He couldn't fix it nor would he try.

"Oh, God, Jim. I'm scared to death. If she was with another man, she would have least had the decency to call me at our appointed hour and pretend everything was okay."

"And?"

"And there's no use speculating because that could go on endlessly."

"So?"

"So, I'm powerless over this."

"Turn it over to ...?"

"I know you'd turn it over to God, but that's not in my toolkit. To the universe, I guess. I love you, man. I know it's late and I got just what I needed. I'll let you get back to bed. Thanks."

"Any time."

Audrey joined me on the deck while I drank coffee. The cats seemed surprised and hung around us. Stars still burned bright against the coal-black sky. Under other conditions it would have been a joy being here. I'm a non-believer, a skeptic, but I wondered about the forces of the universe which had gotten the supermarket clerk out into the parking lot and telling the manager I was there and him choosing to come out and talk to me. If those things hadn't happened, it's very likely I would have drunk that six pack and who knows how much after that.

I closed my eyes and listened to the creek's soft lullaby.

I was driving my old MGB-GT, drunk, when I came around a curve, went off the road, and came back on into the path of another car, forcing it off the road. I ran down the hill and saw Kathy's Infiniti, then a trail of blood, and finally was looking into her eyes. My crying woke me up. I shook uncontrollably, trying to think of what to do next when the phone on the patio table rang. For a second, two, I was immobilized, torn between knowing and unknowing. I picked it off the table and pushed the green button.

"Hello?"

"Hi, honey."

I fought the flow of tears.

"Where are you? I've been worried sick."

"It's okay, hon. I'm in the hospital and I'm fine."

What little adrenaline was left in my system kicked in. I had to control myself so I wouldn't shout, "If you're fine what are you doing in the hospital?"

"I was in a wreck. I whacked my head on the dashboard. Got a cut. Bled. Lost consciousness. Got hauled off to the hospital. They're keeping me here to monitor for concussion symptoms, but so far I don't seem to have any. Just a hell of headache. I was pretty disoriented for a while. They thought maybe I had temporary amnesia but that's gone away. And that's when I remembered to call you."

"I have been so worried. Finally called Jim a little bit ago."

"Sounds like a good move."

"Always. When in doubt, call Jim."

"You're lucky to have him."

"I'm lucky to have you. How long do you think they'll keep you?"

"From the sounds of it, if nothing changes they'll let me go later today. I'm so sorry to have worried you. Oh. A doctor just came in. I'll call you as soon as I know something about my discharge. I love you."

"Are you sure you're okay? I want to see you but if you need to stay—"

"Unless they find out that I did have a concussion I'll be out of here as soon as possible."

Tears were welling up. I didn't know how much longer I could hold them back. I managed to squeeze out, "I love you."

I didn't mention the trip to the supermarket.

**

Bursts of flame azalea blazed among rhododendron on the hillsides bordering Weaver Mountain Road. Sonny escorted me to the house, announcing my arrival from fifty yards out. Queenie stood on the porch as I pulled up.

"Well, well, if it isn't Rick Ryder, private eye, who decides to visit his client," she said, reaching for a hug.

"And it's so good to see you, Queenie. Been out working on behalf of that client. And how are you?"

"If we're gonna chat, take a seat. Just brewed a fresh pot."

Two minutes later she returned with two cups of coffee, some milk and sugar. The temperature couldn't have been more than 72 degrees without a blemish on the blue sky.

"To what do I owe the honor, Ryder?"

"I'll get to that, but I asked first. How are you?"

She leaned back in the rocking chair, her eyes aimed toward the southern mountains.

"Well, Richard. I hate to own up to this, but I seem to be getting older."

"Now there's a shocker," I said and it truly was for her to admit to this reality.

"Yeah. Can't do quite what I used to. Or, maybe I can do it, but it takes longer. Get tired quicker, too."

"Imagine that."

"Who'd have thought. Not me, that's for sure."

"You gonna have to give up some of your activities?"

"Been thinkin' about it. The goats are probably the hardest to keep up with. I hate to lose the milk, though."

"You still making cheese?"

"Yeah. I guess I could let that go. Trade the milk to other cheese makers, keep a little for myself. I really don't think I'd mind doing that. It's the idea that I'm not up to it any more that bothers me."

"Happens, my dear."

"What would you know about it, whippersnapper?"

"I know I like naps more than I used to."

She laughed. "Okay. Back to what brought you up the mountain this morning."

"There are some things that bother me, Ms. Weaver."

"Uh oh. This sounds like serious business."

"It is. I'm still bothered that you kept information from me."

"Ryder, I just told you. I'm an old lady. I forget stuff. Don't know what's important. When you asked before why I didn't tell you that I had known Marcus in a previous life, I really didn't think it mattered."

"You said that you hadn't told me because you thought it might implicate you in ... what happened. That's not the same as thinking it wasn't important. In fact, it could be very important. And then there was the business about the car."

"What business about the car?"

I was about to go off on the woman before it occurred to me that it was possible that she actually didn't remember. Maybe the reason for not telling me things or that things kept changing was because her memory was failing.

"Do you remember that Art Revis came to take Marc's Jaguar home with him?"

"I do. And I remember telling him I thought it would be all right for him to take it."

"But you had no authority to say that."

"It just seemed common sense to me," she huffed. "The

police seem to be done out here and he's gonna inherit it anyway. So, am I a suspect here, Richard, or not?"

"As the cops say, Queenie, everybody's a suspect."

"Why would I have killed him?"

"To keep all the money he had with him from being used to buy up land that would be turned into marijuana plantations."

"Better than a bunch o' McMansions and golf courses."

"They'd clear-cut the land, Queenie. At least now, while it's still illegal, growers have to leave some of the forest intact to mask what they're doing."

"Yeah. I know. I don't like the idea. But you don't really think I'd have killed Marc over that, do you?"

It was a stretch and I told her so.

"So, Ryder, why don't you back off and go lookin' for whoever did do it."

"Ah, that's the Queenie I know and love."

Sonny started barking with his tail wagging. We looked down the road toward the cabin and saw a gray pickup heading toward us.

"SaraJean," Queenie said.

The truck stopped just short of my Honda. Sonny raised the pitch of his greeting until she got out and started roughhousing with him. She was dressed in blue jeans and a dark blue t-shirt, cut off at the shoulders. I hadn't realized how buff she was, and how nicely she filled out her t-shirt. We greeted each other, and SaraJean turned to Queenie.

"Thought I'd come up and help with the cheese."

"Tarnation," Queenie said, "I clean forgot we were doin' that today. You got anything else you need to talk to me about, Ryder? I've just been reminded that I have work to do."

"One thing. Do you know how Art got here from Blacksburg to get the Jaguar?"

"Some friend of his dropped him off."

This was consistent with what we'd heard before.

"Did you meet this friend?"

"No, I didn't. He'd gone on by the time I came out of the house."

"So you didn't see what kind of vehicle he came in."

"That's right."

"Then I suppose that's it. Maybe since I'm out this way, I'll head down to see your brother, SaraJean. I presume he hasn't gone off anywhere."

"Not likely. At least not physically. No tellin' where his mind might be."

Kathy's call came as I was leaving Queenie's.

"The doctor was just in and said I could leave any time."

"You sure you're ready? You don't need any more rest or anything?"

"I'm fine, Rick. Really. Just a little bump on the head. Really."

"Okay, then. If you get to feeling bad just go back to the motel and rest."

"Yes, honey. But I'll be fine. I'll talk to you tonight."

After I'd hung up I realized I hadn't mentioned her accident to Queenie. Maybe I would have if SaraJean hadn't shown up.

On the way down the hill I noted that the crime scene tape at the cabin had fallen into disrepair, still visible but hanging in strips here and there. Maybe it had been cut or maybe the elements had done it in. Whatever, it seemed like an invitation to stop and look around. I took an exam glove from my glove box and slipped it on, a procedure for a one-handed person requiring dexterity and teeth.

The sheriff's people had already been through the place and taken anything of interest, but I poked around inside the cabin anyway, on the "you-never-know" principle. Nothing caught my eye during a twenty minute walk-around. I turned my attention to the outbuilding, not satisfied with Detective Fair's suggestion that Revis might simply have wandered out there after inadvertently overdosing himself with alcohol and sleeping pills.

Queenie referred to the building as the "little barn" to distinguish it from the "big barn" up by the house. It was a combination attic, basement, and garage. I imagined that everything on the property that was once useful but had fallen into disrepair was stored there. Old farm implements, a bicycle, a couple of lawn mowers, a chainsaw, shelves of old magazines, rusty tools hanging on the walls. At first glance, it appeared to be lot of clutter. A closer look revealed an order to it. Hand tools over here, power equipment there, lawn stuff over in a corner. There were probably hidden treasures in there, but it was just as likely that one or more variety of vermin had set up household among the detritus. I ventured through the door near which Revis's body was found, now not taped nor even pulled close. The chalk outline of the corpse was still visible. It looked like a body stretched out on the ground with arms up, over its head. Standing in the doorway on my way out, I glanced back at the white drawing on the floor. Turning to fully face the body's outline, I imagined myself coming into this place and falling, unconscious, passing out. I wondered if I would fall fully stretched out or would simply slump to the ground, in a more twisted position, more curled up. Did Revis wander alone into this place or did someone lay down his already unconscious body? The latter possibility challenged the notion that he had committed suicide which, in turn, would confirm for us that we were on the right track looking for a murderer.

Crossing the bridge to the Pressley property, I hoped that Arlo's mood had improved since my last visit. A knock on the front door got me a "Come!" followed by "Hey, y'ol' son-of-a-bitch. Where you been hidin'?"

"Out in plain sight. How you been doin'?"

"Any worse and you could just drop me in a hole."

"That's what I like. A positive spirit. Saw your sister up at Queenie's. She's looking good. Well-toned, like she'd been lifting weights."

"Comes from slingin' bales of hay up there. She's always been a physical lass. Too bad she doesn't like men very much. She'd be a good catch for someone."

"What about another woman?" I asked, knowing I was approaching a boundary.

"Huh? Like a lesbo? My sister?"

"You can't tell me it's never occurred to you."

"Yeah, I've thought about it. What I really wonder about is how much my bein' around hasn't gotten in the way of all that. Man or woman."

I didn't have a ready response.

"Oh, man," Arlo said. "Look at me. What a lousy host. There's some coffee in one a' them carafe things in the kitchen. You could help yourself you wanted some."

"I'm okay. Had some up at Queenie's."

"Queenie Weaver, Queen of the Mountain. How is the old gal these days?"

"Thinks she's gettin' old."

"Queenie? She'll outlive the rest of us. Now there's a

woman needs a man."

"Seems to have done okay so far without one."

"I guess. She and my sister. I guess they're like sisters, too. They fight, make up, fight, make up. It's like a soap opera I get to watch live, better'n the TV. Got some good ganja here, but I imagine you'll pass, Mr. Recovery."

"I'm not sure if you think that's a good thing or a bad thing."

"Oh, I don't know, Rick. Sometimes my innate cynicism gets the better of me. I think it's probably a very good thing. Go through life with a clear head. I can't remember the last time I thought mine was straight. Back when I was a kid, I guess. Havin' your fuckin' legs shot off doesn't help, tho'."

His gaze went off into the middle distance to a place I couldn't imagine.

"I'm about to fire up this bad boy," he said, holding up a fat joint, "and watch Blazing Saddles. Ever see that movie?"

"Oh, yeah. Several times."

"Cracks you up every time, don't it?"

"It's a pretty funny movie," I agreed.

"You know that guy, what's his name, took all that vitamin C when he had the cancer? One who recommended watchin' funny movies to treat it? Marx Brothers, all those old ones. Who was that guy? A writer, I think."

"Norman Cousins," I said.

"Yeah. That's the guy. Anyway, I thought I'd see how it does for havin' no pegs, you know. Might help my mood, which, as my lovely sister is wont to suggest, could use some general improvement."

"Couldn't hurt, I wouldn't think."

"So, want to join me?"

What I thought Arlo needed as much as anything was

companionship, and I was torn between staying and sharing a few good laughs with the man and getting on with my own work. I came down on the 'what the hell' side of it.

"Sure."

"No shit?"

"No shit."

An hour and a half later, my mood greatly improved, I said I really did need to get going, that I was still trying to earn a living.

***

With nothing particular on the agenda and my mind behaving as if it were wandering through molasses and the weather being what it was, I decided to take Anne McDonald up on her suggestion to visit Celo. Given the Peters and Ryder bias that face-to-face conversations tend to be more fruitful than the long-distance kind, I thought I might learn more than I had talking with her on the phone. The decision got me back in sleuth mode.

As if I'd teleported my thoughts to Colorado, Kathy called while I was having a burger at a fast food place in Burnsville.

"I heard a different point of view about the professor from a young woman I spoke to."

"The one the Wyatt guy—"

"Wyans."

"Yeah. The woman he referred you to?"

"No. I meet her in about half an hour. This is someone else. She'd heard I was here gathering information about Marc and knew that a lot of people around here have negative ideas about him and she wanted me to know that wasn't everyone's experience. She'd been a student and research assistant with him. According to her, he was nothing but supportive. He mentored her while she was working on her PhD and helped her get an article published from her thesis. She thought he was kind of flirty but never did anything out of the way—those were her words, 'out of the way'—with her."

"How did she get hold of you?"

"Dr. Wyans gave her my number."

"Did he know she'd give Revis a positive review?"

"I don't know. She told me she asked him for it and he couldn't very well turn her down."

"Do you think her experiences change anything?"

"I don't know. But apparently he wasn't a complete asshole all the time."

***

The Celo Community is nestled in the hills below Mount Mitchell, the highest peak east of the Mississippi, and refers to itself as a "communal settlement." A quick internet search revealed there were some forty households living on its twelve hundred acres. I hadn't called in advance: I figured that, if Anne wasn't home, I'd drive on up to the state park at the top of the mountain, making a full day of the trip; if she was, I'd at have the element of surprise on my side.

Fortune smiled. She was home and invited me out. The porch provided a panoramic view of the valley below. She was in her mid-sixties, dressed casually in khaki walking shorts and a shirt decorated with flowers embroidered on the front. Her platinum hair was short and brushed back over her ears.

After serving iced tea—the ubiquitous southern drink—she said, "I don't know what I can tell you that I didn't tell you before."

"Nor do I. I imagine you've seen those detective shows where the sleuth bumbles along until he or she comes across something interesting."

"Columbo," she said.

"Precisely."

Her gaze held steady on my face before she said, "I'm not sure if this is indelicate, but may I ask what happened to your arm?"

"Of course," I said. "It happened in a car wreck when I was eighteen."

I'd always preferred that people ask outright so they're not thinking about it the entire time I'm in their company. The 'elephant in the room' kind of thing. But I often wonder just how much to share. This seemed to be one of those times when more would be okay.

"I was driving drunk. A girl my age, died."

"That's terrible."

"It was, yes. And life altering. It took me only ten years to quit drinking afterwards."

Her expression was the one people get when they don't know what to say.

"Some of us are slow learners," I added.

"Some of the best learning comes over time."

"If you live through it."

She smiled. "Yes, of course, there's that." She sipped her drink. "So you're here to bumble around?"

"Not too much. But we don't seem be getting closer to understanding what happened to Marc out at that cabin. My wife talked with a former student of his who had nice things to say about him: he was very supportive of her work, helped her get published, that kind of thing. To tell the truth, it was … different from the kinds of things we'd heard up till then."

"'Her'," Anne said. "And a good-looking 'her' I imagine. He was a womanizer, Mr. Ryder. He was helpful with students, if they were smart and attractive. And they loved him. As far as I know he never acted inappropriately with any of them. I mean, I never heard anything about him making unwanted sexual advances toward his students. They just helped him maintain his ego. And in exchange he helped them advance their careers. Besides, there were plenty of opportunities to engage in the 'wanted' kind."

"What about the notion that he took credit for work his students had done?"

"That's hardly earthshaking news in the academic world. Students always think professors steal their work. To some degree it's true. Articles get published all the time showing the professor as the lead author, followed by the others who worked on it. The professor often has done little of the work, if any. And Marc did have a real problem giving proper attribution." After a millisecond of thought she added, "Unless you were an attractive female student and had the right, shall we say, appreciation for him. Not a new story, unfortunately."

"Would there have been students of his, current or former, who would have been at the conference in Asheville?"

"I would imagine."

"Any with enough of a grudge to murder him?"

"It seems unlikely. But I guess you never know with people, do you? I felt like killing him a few times myself."

After Anne poured more iced tea into plastic tumblers, we took a walking tour of Celo. When we got back to her house, I said it was time for me to go. One never knows if these things are projections but I sensed I would have been welcome to stay indefinitely. It led me to speculate about what she might have been doing while Professor Revis was "encouraging" his young female students.

***

The call came at 10:02. Any later and I would have had to call Jim again.

She said she was feeling fine and would be on the seven o'clock plane out of Denver in the morning. If all went as scheduled, she'd arrive in Asheville at 2:00 p.m.

"About the second woman you interviewed," I prompted.

"I think you'll find this very interesting. Her name's Cheri Ballard, and she rode with Professor Revis to Asheville. She was to make a presentation based on a paper they'd co-authored. She seemed a little testy about that since, according to her, she'd done most of the work and all the writing. He'd reviewed the paper and made a suggestion or two that she incorporated but she didn't think that arose to the level of co-authorship. But here's the really interesting part."

"I'm all ears."

"She made the keynote address in Revis's absence."

"Say what?"

"I think you heard me. She made the keynote address at the conference after Revis was… after he didn't show up."

"Wow!"

"Exactly what I thought."

"How'd that come about?"

"She convinced the program director—Dr. Philips—that she was familiar enough with the material that she could do it. In fact, she had a copy of his presentation slides."

"That can't have been harmful to her professional reputation."

"She wasn't reluctant to speak to that, about how it was a

lucky break for her. Yes, of course, tragic for Professor Revis. But life goes on."

"Or doesn't, as the case may be. Would you describe the woman as attractive?"

"Quite. Why?"

"I talked with the ex-wife this afternoon. Apparently, the professor was quite helpful to attractive young women. She was circumspect in how she talked about it, but I got the inference that occasionally, if not frequently, there was a quid pro quo."

"Sex."

"Yes. Made for a difficult marriage. I guess the guy was ... well, we know he was brilliant and could be very charming."

"Was Ms. McDonald ever a student of his?"

"Never occurred to me to ask. Although she also is quite attractive and has a quick mind herself. Good work, Ms. Peters. I wonder if the cops know about this Ballard woman."

"And thank you for your vote of confidence, Mr. Ryder. Someone else to add to our ever-expanding suspect list, do you suppose?"

"I would like to know where she was from nine to ten o'clock or so on the night Revis died. Did Ms. Ballard happen to say anything about the money?"

"She said she'd heard the rumors but that Revis never talked about it."

"You're riding with someone about whom there are rumors that he has a million or so dollars somewhere and the subject never comes up? Did she happen to say if she heard these rumors before or after he died?"

"She didn't." After a moment's silence, Kathy asked, "Are you still there?"

"Yeah. Conjuring up scenarios. One in which she and Philips are in cahoots."

"How do you see that playing out?"

"Not sure. I'll call Detective Fair tomorrow. See if they know anything about Ms. Ballard. Maybe talk to Philips again, ask him why he didn't bother to mention the woman."

"Just don't forget to pick me up."

"Two o'clock," I said, displaying my command of the situation.

It wasn't until I'd turned the lights off for the night that I thought about her dinner with the Wyans guy. I supposed that was a good sign.

Seven

Wednesday

A cold front came in overnight, harbinger of a change of season. I wore a sweatshirt while on the deck with my early morning coffee, Audrey at my feet, the cats off to who knew where. Scrutinizing our newly updated list of possibilities, I moved the Ballard-Philips scenario to the top. They both stood to benefit from the professor's demise, especially if they found the bankroll. The pair could have gone to the cabin. It wouldn't have mattered if Revis was there or not. If they were there when he arrived they'd say something like, Surprise! Thought we'd come out for a visit. He might have been suspicious, but after another bourbon and another joint everything would be cool. Having accompanied the professor overland, presumably with two or more overnight stays, the woman would very likely know about, and have had access to, the sleeping pills. Or at least she would have known he had them and where he kept them. At the cabin, she doses another drink with more of the meds. He passes out. They carry him to the outbuilding. Maybe they didn't intend to kill him; merely wanted him out of the way while they looked for the money. Or, one or the other of them knew where it was; maybe the professor talked about it. I placed my bet on the girl learning the whereabouts of the cash while on their cross-county journey. Pillow talk.

It was too early to call the Buncombe County Sheriff's Department, but after all this heavy-duty speculating, I was ready to talk to Detective Fair. Instead, I returned to the kitchen and whipped up a breakfast drink and read the morning paper. Satisfied that the Republic was still intact and no one had subverted county or city government for another day, I made my call.

"Fair," the detective greeted me in his laid-back way after I'd been forwarded to him.

"Ryder here. Can you spare a minute to talk about the Revis case?"

"What do you have?"

"It's more like what do you have, Detective? For instance, do you know about the woman, Cheri Ballard, who rode with the professor from Colorado?"

I could almost hear the gears in his mind grinding. "Yes."

"That was terse, Detective. Is she a suspect?"

"I'm afraid you've misunderstood me, Ryder. There are no active suspects. We are not investigating this case at this time."

"Still a suicide?"

"Or, accidental overdose. Anything else?"

I was crestfallen. I'd let myself believe than this would be new information for which the detective would be grateful, helping them see the case in a new light. As Kathy is wont to remind me, my ego tends to get the best of me at times. I thought about filling him in on my conversation with Anne McDonald but accepted that there wasn't anything that would change his perspective on the matter.

"Guess that's it," I said with a muffled sigh of resignation.

"Okay. Call again. Any time. You keep at this, you might find something useful."

"I believe that's what's called a left-handed compliment, Detective."

"Sorry. I really do appreciate your willingness to share what you've found with us, Ryder. Not always true with you private dicks."

"We aim to please, Detective."

"Uh-huh."

At 9:00 a.m. I was aware that Kathy would have boarded the plane for home. To my great relief, there'd been nothing on the news yesterday or this morning about airplane "incidents" to raise my anxiety beyond its normal level when she traveled without me.

At my favorite bookstore I got a latte, set up shop, and revisited the suspect list.

- Cheri Ballard and Professor Philips—greed, and retribution for how they'd been treated.
- Queenie—outrage at what he was planning to do with the money.
- Art Revis—revenge for his unhappy childhood and money to make up for what he would not inherit.
- Ann McDonald—because he was an asshole; maybe also for the money.
- Art and Anne collectively for the above-enumerated reasons.

I tried to envision a scenario in which Queenie was involved. I couldn't, in spite of my standard "you-never-know-what-people-are-capable-of" refrain. She even liked the guy—although she could have put that out there as a smoke screen.

The more I thought about the Ballard-Philips scenario, the more I liked it. They could have hatched the scheme before she and the professor left Colorado, maybe as soon as one or the other of them found out about the money.

It was too late for Kathy to go back and interview Cheri again, but I could revisit Philips. My recollection was that he'd be in the area for the rest of the week before heading back to Chapel Hill. I didn't have time to see him before collecting Kathy from the airport. She'd have to accompany me. When I called, he made no reference to the condition he was in the last time we parted. He agreed to meet us for drinks at 3:00, assuming her flight was on time.

The butterflies in my stomach had me on the edge of nausea. I'd bought a small bouquet because I wanted her to have something pretty and holding it gave me something to do with my hand. The extra fifteen minutes I had allowed myself to get to the airport were unneeded: the arrivals board showed that flight had been delayed. It was now scheduled to land at 3:30. I called Philips to ask if he'd be okay with meeting at 4:00. I thought I detected minor annoyance in his voice, but he agreed to the change.

I almost didn't recognize her as she came through the gate wearing a big slouch hat covering most of her face. We hugged and cried for a minute. When she took the hat off I saw the bandage on her forehead. Not huge, but bigger than your average boo-boo cover. On the way to the baggage claim, after determining she was feeling no ill effects from the accident, I told her about my plan to meet with Professor Philips and asked if she was okay with that—or if she'd rather get home and rest.

"It's okay, really. I got some meds for pain and actually slept on the plain. Just don't expect me to be a vital part of the conversation," she warned.

Philips was seated in a booth, a half-drunk pint of beer in front of him. I imagined it was not his first. He greeted us warmly, said it was a pleasure to meet Kathy.

After ordering our drinks, and ping-ponging the requisite meaningless chit-chat, I said, "We're hoping you can help us, Randy. We're stuck. We don't seem to be getting anywhere with this."

"Maybe there's nowhere to get," he said. "Maybe it's what they've said it was—suicide or accidental overdose."

"How do you explain the missing money?" Kathy asked.

Philips looked surprised, as if he hadn't expected Kathy to be active in this conversation. "I don't think he had it. I think that was rumor and speculation. I wouldn't doubt that there are people, organizations, whatever, who would support him—or anyone—in buying up land on speculation assuming that, sooner or later, it will become legal to grow marijuana in this state. But I really doubt that Dr. Revis had that money."

Now it was my turn. "I'm confused, Randy. When you and I first met, you told me that Marc had told you about the money and how he had brought it out here although he wouldn't tell you where it was."

"He did. And the more I've thought about it the more I've come to believe that was just another story he was telling to make himself important. You know he did that kind of thing."

"So we've heard," Kathy said. "We've also heard about Cheri Ballard."

His face went blank. No surprise. No question. Nothing.

"You do know her, don't you?" Kathy asked.

"Yes. Of course. I just don't know why her name would come up in a conversation about Marc's death."

"Well," I began, "she did ride out here with him from

Colorado. Is that right?"

"Yes, but ... "

"She was a protégée of his, correct?"

"Yes."

"She gave the keynote address after his, how might you put it, untimely unavailability?"

"Yes, she did."

"I know you've said you don't think there was any large sum of cash, but if there had been, would it not be reasonable to assume that, after riding together three days, or however long it took them, she would know about it and know where it was?"

"Like I said, I don't think ... "

I held my hand up in the universal stop sign. "Yes. We know what you said."

"What is this? It feels like you're interrogating me. 'Didn't I know this?' 'Wouldn't I know that?' I've told you all I know."

"Except you didn't tell me about Cheri," I said.

"I told you I didn't think it was important. You know, I didn't come here to get the third degree. I thought I was doing you a courtesy. Now you're making it out like I'm the one who's done something wrong. Why don't you go on back to Asheville." He stood, threw a ten dollar bill on the table, said, "That'll cover my beer and a tip," turned and walked away.

Kathy and I exchanged well, wasn't that interesting looks.

"Methinks the professor doth protest too much," she said.

"Likewise. So, where do we go from here?"

"How about home. I'm beat."

When we were on the highway, I said, "So this woman who holds a grudge against Revis nonetheless rides across the country with him."

"And intimated that they had a good time in spite of their

history."

"Yeah. Well, she probably wouldn't say anything other than that if she'd been planning on killing the guy."

"True."

"Seems to me the money is the smoking gun here."

"You mean, whoever has it is the perpetrator. Meaning also that we have to find it."

"I'm not sure what more we're likely to turn up by interviewing these people."

"Suppose it would do any good to talk to Randy Philips's associates at UNC?" she asked.

"I don't know. Unlike Revis, Philips is still alive. People may not be as willing to talk straight about him."

"Oh, come on, Rick. We're investigators. How good are we if we only get people who want to talk to be candid. I thought we did a good job with Philips."

"You mean chasing him away?"

"Didn't you see the guilt written all over him? He's implicated in something. Maybe not murder, but something."

"What is there besides murder?"

"My gosh! Have you forgotten how we do things? We don't have to have the answers in order to continue asking the questions."

"Point taken. Who's going to go to Chapel Hill?"

Before we were able to answer that question, the phone rang. I told the car to answer.

"Mr. Ryder? This is Angie with S&S Security. Is anyone in your house at the moment?"

My stomach dropped. These were the people who provided our home alarm system.

"No. My wife and I are both in the car. We're around Mills River, on our way home."

"Your alarm has gone off, sir. Do you want me to contact the sheriff?"

***

I did my best to keep the Honda under 65 on the interstates on the way to the house. Kathy kept telling me to take it easy, repeating that no matter how fast I drove the sheriff's people would be there before we arrived. I practiced my deep breathing. It was dusk as we approached Riceville Road, which was a challenge to drive even in broad daylight. I almost lost it on the first S curve.

"Stop!"

"What?"

She repeated, "Stop. Pull over."

I pulled into the next driveway. "What's the matter?"

"Your driving is the matter. You are going to get us killed. If you don't slow down, I'm walking home. I'm not kidding!"

I knew she wasn't.

"You do realize that I was in a car accident a little while ago, don't you? Do you have any idea what your crazy driving is doing to me? Get it together. I mean it."

She sat back in her seat, hands in her lap, staring straight ahead.

"God, I'm so sorry. I am such a jerk."

"Yes, you are."

The rest of the way home I maintained the speed limit—less on the dicier parts of the road. Strobing blue and white lights were visible before we reached the house. Eric and a deputy were on the front stoop.

"You the neighborhood welcoming committee?" I asked as we approached.

Audrey came bounding around from the back of the house, giving us his usual, "Oh-my-gosh-I-can't-believe-you're-back!" presentation. I saw a red line down the middle of his back. It was blood.

"Jeee-sus. What happened to you, buddy?" I asked.

"He probably let himself out through the hole in the broken glass door."

I looked closely. Beneath the blood I could see a gash down his midline.

"You okay, boy?"

The way he jumped and wriggled convinced me he was.

"Rick, Kathy," Eric intervened. "This is Deputy Harry Norton." He nodded toward the uniform.

"Mr. Ryder. Mrs. Ryder. There has been a break-in. I've searched the house. No one's inside and nothing has been obviously disrupted. Although obviously you're going to have to do a thorough search yourselves to see if anything's missing. I'll be glad to walk with you through the house."

"How'd they get in?" I asked.

"Broke the glass in one of the sliding doors on the back deck. Like I said, that's probably what your dog cut himself on."

I unlocked the front door and we all trudged in.

"I need a—" I caught myself before I said, "a drink," although it was the first thing that came to mind, a reminder that I was sober, not cured. "A cup of coffee. Anybody else?"

"I'll have a glass of wine," Kathy said. "And you don't need to skimp."

The deputy took me up on the coffee offer.

"Have a beer?" Eric asked.

"Afraid not. White wine is the best I can do in the spirits department."

He shrugged and agreed that would be fine.

We sat around the dining room table where we got a close-up of the broken glass door. A large rock lay on the floor. A line of blood led from a hanging shard onto the deck.

"I heard the alarm go off," Eric said. "I thought about coming over to check things out, but I wasn't sure I wanted to come across burglars in the act so I just watched from the edge of the property. I know you have a security company and figured they'd be dealing with it. I did think it strange that there was no vehicle around. When the cruiser came up I walked over, was about halfway up the drive when I saw a gray pickup come down out of the forest road. I'm sure it was the same one I saw the other day. I got the license plate number."

Deputy Norton looked back and forth between us. "Something happen recently?"

"A few days ago when Kathy and I were both gone Eric saw a couple of guys walking around the house. Said they were there to do some work for me. Not true."

"You report it?" the Norton asked.

"There didn't seem much to report."

"Excuse me," Kathy said. "I'm going to bed. It's been a long day. I can't deal with anything else, I'm afraid."

"I'm done, too," Norton said. "You'll need to come down tomorrow to file your own report. Make sure you do a good inventory to see if anything's been messed with or is missing."

I thanked him and as he was leaving, Eric said, "I guess my work here is done, as well."

"Thanks for keeping your eyes on things," I said. "Really. It's nice to know that someone's paying attention."

"Are you involved in anything your neighbors should know about?" He asked, holding a tight grin and raised eyebrows.

"Well, we are investigating something that might involve a lot of money."

"Might?"

"We've heard competing stories."

"But it's possible someone wants to know what you know," he said.

"Or wants us to leave it alone."

"Interesting work you two do."

"Keeps us off the streets," I said.

After the others were gone, I went back upstairs to see how Kathy was. She was in bed with a book.

"You okay?"

"Yes. Really, I am. And I'm over being mad at you. You go on back and deal with all this stuff, okay. Really. I'm exhausted. And I do love you. Even if you are an ass at times. You can turn of the light."

"Now there's an endorsement."

We exchanged a gentle kiss, I doused the light, and went on downstairs. I called a 24-hour glass-repair service, knowing it would cost a small fortune to have someone come out at that time of night, but I wasn't comfortable going to bed with the place unsecured. There was no point in setting the alarm and, although I'm not entirely a klutz, a temporary patch to the window would involve more that my one hand could handle. While waiting for the repair people to arrive I turned my sleuth mind to the break-in.

Cove Road ends at the far edge of our property which abuts the national forest. A sign where the road turns off from Riceville Road informs travelers that the paved road ends in one and a half miles. From there on, it's gravel as it wends its way up the mountain until it runs into the Blue Ridge Parkway. Little traffic goes up there with the exception of people out for a drive who are curious about where it goes or whose GPS tells them they can get to the Parkway that way. Although it is a county road, it is clearly not a priority item on their maintenance list. People who unknowingly adventure onto it rarely do so twice.

So. What was the gray pickup doing parked there? I let that question stew while I tended to the hound. It appeared that, indeed, he had climbed through the hole left by the rock, cutting himself in the process. He gave out a few yips when I cleaned the wound but generally was grateful for the attention.

The glass people left about 1:00 a.m. I was still wired. While lying in bed pondering possibilities, I came up with a scenario. What if? The burglars—or whatever they are—come out to reconnoiter the place and check out our security arrangement. They're interrupted by Eric but have found out what they need to know. These boys are not clever enough to figure how to disable the thing, so the next time—yesterday—they come back to find out how much time they would have to carry out whatever nefarious plan they have in mind after the alarm is set off and before law enforcement responds. They park where the car won't be seen, go around the house, throw the rock through the door, go back to their car, wait to see how long it takes for the deputy to arrive, then drive off.

If—and I knew this was a big if—I had the thing figured out, there was another step in their plan.

Eight

Thursday

The morning was gloomy, overcast, and chilly, fitting our states of mind. I sat at the kitchen table rather than out on the deck with my coffee. Audrey lay near my feet, perhaps on the misguided assumption that this was some kind of meal from which he would benefit sooner or later. The cats had yet to return from their nocturnal prowling. I called Teddy Riddle, our source for checking license plate numbers before I delivered Kathy's tea.

"How worried do you think we should be?" she asked.

"I believe they'll be back. I think we need to have outside cameras installed."

She shivered. "Makes me nervous. What do your detective instincts tell you they were doing out here?"

I propounded my theory about their two trips being exploratory and that we could expect another one. "I think they're either trying to scare us off the case or they're planning to break in and look through our stuff to see if they can find out what we know about the money. Somehow they know when we're away."

"Couldn't these incidents be unrelated to the Revis case? Just some random thieves who are picking on the house at the end of a virtually dead end road?"

"Could. But I doubt it. I hope we'll be able to find a connection between the owners of the truck and what it was doing out here."

I was back in the kitchen pondering breakfast possibilities when my phone rang.

"RJ Enterprises." Teddy was a man of few words.

"Address is a PO box?" I suggested.

"You've got it."

"Give it to me anyway," I said. "We'll check to see whose names are on the incorporation documents."

I grabbed a banana and went up to the office. A call to Secretary of State's Office, where such papers are filed, yielded three names: Rodney A. Calhoun; Jason C. Calhoun; and, Carrie F. Calhoun. Rodney was shown as the principal agent. The location of the business was in the Asheville Business Park, a small office complex on the perimeter of downtown.

The phone number shown for the business was, unsurprisingly, not a working number. All three people used the same PO address.

"Guess we'll have to drive to town and see what's there. Want to go in and have breakfast?"

"I'd rather stay put," she said. "I'm still hungover from jet lag and the excitement on the way home."

I presumed she was also still suffering the effects of the accident she'd been in and hoped that the experts were right in declaring that she hadn't had a concussion.

"Okay. I'll zip in and fix something to eat when I come back. Shouldn't take long, the place is right off Tunnel Road."

The drive took less than ten minutes. The directory showed that RJ Enterprises were in office 203 on the second floor. The only identification for that space was a business card stuck in the lower left corner of a frosted window. It showed the name of the business and this address, nothing I didn't already know. As I expected would be the case, there was no response to my knock. I assumed nobody actually occupied the office, that it was used only when some official document required a physical location rather than a post office box number.

Back home, I sliced a couple of fresh sausage links into a skillet, fried them until they were brown, scrambled a few eggs and dumped them into the pan, sprinkled a little dried parsley and thyme over it all, stirred in some shredded cheddar cheese until it was a gooey mess, and served it with fresh wheat toast.

Kathy's internet search of the three principals was our topic of conversation while we ate.

"Apparently, Rodney Calhoun is married to Carrie. I'm guessing that Jason is a brother, given that their ages are two years apart. Could be a cousin, nephew, whatever, I suppose. Anyway, of interest is that Rodney and Carrie were busted for growing pot back in 2003. He was sentenced to three months in prison. The charges against her were dropped to misdemeanor possession which was suspended since it was a first offense."

"Hmm. Pot growers. My, my. How the plot thickens. Or, the pot boils, as it were."

"Clever. So ... it would seem that some local pot producers have an interest in our investigation. Perhaps they, like some law enforcement officers, want to keep people from buying land for marijuana production in this area. Albeit for different reasons."

"These people don't want the competition," I suggested.

"You don't suppose there are marijuana growers who get help from those very same law enforcers who claim to be opposed to what they're doing?"

"I'm shocked, my dear, simply shocked, that you would even suggest such a thing."

"Well," she said, as she leaned toward me, lowering her voice conspiratorially. "I understand such things went on during prohibition, when certain moonshiners were able to curry favor with the local constabulary by, oh, one hates to say it, but by, what? Profit sharing?"

"The maintenance of an illicit mood-altering drug manufacturing culture is a time-honored practice in the mountains. You ever see Thunder Road with Robert Mitchum?"

"Can't say I have."

"What! It's a classic about moonshining. Filmed right around here."

"Maybe we should watch it. Good eggs, dear. Sure you don't want to get out of the sleuthing game and open a restaurant?"

"Actually, I would love to have a little diner. Serve breakfast and lunch. But it would be the same menu for both. Unfortunately, real diners are no longer chic. You know, that one in West Asheville was bought and turned into an upscale burger place. Just what the city needs."

"I get it. We're gonna keep on as private eyes. Suits me."

When we'd finished eating, Kathy said, "I know I was flip about the corruption, but doesn't it disturb you that this goes on?"

"If you recall my professional history, dear, you will remember that I investigated big-time pollution in this state, the kind of thing that can't go on without some kind of high-level official protection. Higher than the local sheriff. Our most recent ex-governor used to be an executive for one of the major violators of environmental regulations in the Southeast."

Kathy closed her eyes. When she opened them, she said, "I get it about political sleaze. I'm not sure I'm clear about what the Calhouns might be up to. They, or their agents, come to our house to back us off our investigation. Do you suppose they could have been responsible for Marc's death?"

"For the sake of conversation, let's assume whoever our two visitors report to are involved in that. Isn't it ironic that we wouldn't even be on to them if they hadn't sent those two yahoos out here?"

"But they don't know that we aren't on to them," she said. "They think we're these hot-shot investigators and we'll discover their involvement with Dr. Revis' demise unless they get us to stop our work. And, if they have the money, that's more reason to keep the sleuths away. So they send these stooges out to scare us off." She took a breath before adding, "How do these bozos know when we're not home?"

I squeezed my lips together. If I'd had a mustache it would have twitched. "They've been staking us out. There're lots of places out this way where someone hiding could see us coming but where we wouldn't see them."

"You mean they just sit there all day until they think we've gone. Both of us?"

"They might not be there all the time. Maybe they work eight to five. A regular gig. It's not so far-fetched. They come out early enough to see if we leave home."

"Really. Just on the random chance that we'll both be gone at the same time."

"What's so hard to imagine about that? That's the kind of thing we do, isn't it? That's what you just did hanging around the Marotti house to see when she was leaving."

"Right. Okay. What do we do now?"

"We've got to fool them into thinking that we're both gone when one of us is still here."

"How do we do that?"

"We could make a dummy and put it in the passenger seat."

"A dummy," she repeated, the word weighted with skepticism.

"Stay with me here. Do you remember a few years back when some prisoners up at Craggy Prison did that? They stuffed a bunch of paper into a set of prison clothes to make a dummy so someone could escape from a work crew. Got away with it, too. They didn't find out the guy was gone till morning bed check."

"So who'll be our dummy?"

We looked at each other and, like we'd had fuses lit in us, burst out laughing. There was no doubt who our dummy would be.

Nine

Friday

We sat at the dining room table stuffing a pair of slacks and a one-sleeved shirt with newspaper, rolled up a head-sized ball and stuck a cap on it. From several feel away, especially looking at it from the driver's side of Kathy's Infiniti, it could easily pass for a passenger. Kathy's job was to make a round-trip to the nearby shopping center, keeping an eye out for the gray pickup parked off the road and to call me if she saw it. Whether she called or not, I'd be waiting in the living room.

In preparation for any possible confrontation, I retrieved my .38 Smith and Wesson revolver from the basement gun case. Although I thought it was no more than a 50-50 likelihood that either of them would be armed—it didn't seem like they'd been making that kind of visit—you never know.

Seven minutes after pulling out of the drive she called. "They were parked alongside the community center. If I hadn't been looking for them, I'd have missed them. They should be there in a couple of minutes. Don't do anything stupid, okay?"

"Who? Me?"

"Yeah. The guy who shot a hole in the living room wall bein' all macho and stuff."

"You're gonna keep bringing that up for the rest our lives

together, aren't you?"

"You better believe it. It's good ammunition, staying with the shooting analogy."

"Okay. I'm getting myself steeled, ready for the bad guys. When you come back, park tight in back of them so they have to do some maneuvering to get out."

Two minutes later, Audrey initiated his early-warning racket. I got him to join me on the couch where I sat with the .38 in my lap while he strained at his collar, ready to protect the household.

The dummy had worked. They didn't try to hide their presence, presumably on the assumption that no one was home. I heard them coming up the steps to the back deck. Without any to-do, another large rock crashed through one of the newly replaced glass doors. They'd apparently given up any thought of subtlety and were into direct action. The alarm went off. A hand came through where glass had been, unlocked the door, slid it open. Eric's descriptions of the two men were perfect. By then, Audrey had broken my hold on his collar and was going berserk. I saw a gun aimed at him. I fired mine before they could shoot the dog, shattering the rest of the door glass.

"Hello, gentlemen," I said. They exchanged a look and began to turn as if to leave. I fired another shot, this one into the space where the glass door had been. Adrenaline is a drug that depresses common sense and I do get a little carried away when I have a gun in my hand. "Stay where you are. Now, turn toward me. Put your weapons down slowly and put your hands behind your heads. Now!"

They were compliant.

A car turned into the drive.

"I believe that would be my wife. And I'm gonna be in deep doo-doo since you incited me to go all postal. She gets really testy when I shoot this thing in the house," I said, waving the revolver around like a maniac in a Quentin Tarantino film.

"Anyway," I continued, "you hear that alarm? We're just gonna let it go, and in a moment my phone's gonna ring. That'll be the security company. I'm sure you saw the sign out front. And we're gonna let it ring because then the security company will call the sheriff. My guess is that you counted on that. Except for the part with me being here. You assumed that breaking the door would set off the alarm and that you would have time to do whatever it is you came to do—probably shoot the dog, the cats, too, if they were around. You knew that after no one answered the call from the security company, they would call the sheriff, and then a car would be dispatched. Ten minutes at least before anyone showed up, probably more like fifteen, twenty. So now I have a choice. I can go ahead and let the law come on out here and get you two bozos for trespassing, breaking and entering an occupied dwelling, firearms violations, whatever else we can conjure up. Or, I can call the security people and tell them everything's okay and they can call off the cops."

Pony Tail said, "Man, we wasn't gonna hurt nothin'. Really. Just wanted to scare you off, you know?"

"No, I actually don't know. Why don't you tell me. Scare me off what?"

Neither of them spoke, and I was about to go into another gun-waving frenzy when the phone rang.

"Time's a'wastin', boys. Gonna tell me what's goin' on here?"

"We heard about you, man," the one with the loose hair said. "You're crazy."

I smiled. "I'm glad I've been able to maintain my reputation," I said, wondering how these low-life employees of pot growers came to hear about me.

I heard the car door slam. Kathy would be upstairs in two minutes or less. It was then that I decided to let the events they had set in motion take their course. That way, when the sheriff arrived it would take her attention off my role in finishing off the door.

"So, you workin' for the Calhouns," I said.

The brief exchange of glances between the two miscreants confirmed my assumption.

"What I don't know is why we are of such interest to you people. I think y'all have had something to do with Professor Revis's untimely passage from this earthly realm. Isn't that how they say it in the obituaries? Gone to his Maker? Went home to be with Jesus?"

Kathy came into the kitchen, took a couple of steps and looked into the living room.

"What happened here?" she asked, waving a hand in the direction of what, until a few moments before, had been a set of perfectly functional and attractive and doubly expensive sliding glass doors.

"Breaking and entering," I said. "These two gentlemen have just confirmed to my satisfaction that they are in the employ of the Calhoun clan. What I'm trying to glean from them now is why they're so interested in us."

"Smells like a gun's been fired in here."

I shrugged. "Yeah. Well, after they smashed the door, this guy—"I pointed at Pony Tail—"was about to shoot Audrey, so I had to distract him."

She shook her head.

We heard the siren. Good timing, I thought.

"You're not off the hook, you know," she said.

"You're that one-armed private eye," the sheriff's deputy said when he came into the living room. His name plate read, "Deputy Arch Edgerton."

"That would be me," I said. "And, this is my wife, Kathy Peters."

"Ma'am," he said, nodding toward her. She nodded in return.

"And these two gentlemen ... " I began to say.

"Oh, I know these characters. And I wouldn't call 'em gentlemen. Daryl? Johnson? What're you guys up to today?"

They didn't respond.

"I believe I've rendered them speechless," I said. "I have, however, determined that they are in the employ of some Calhouns."

The deputy nodded but said nothing, like he knew but couldn't say he knew. "Can't help noticing that door over there. That have anything to do with the call from the security people?"

"Everything," I said, and went on to narrate the events leading up to his arrival, including my part in the mayhem.

"You'll need you to come down to headquarters to make a statement," Edgerton said as Kathy and I followed him with the now-handcuffed villains in tow.

"These guys aren't Calhouns themselves are they?" I asked.

"These two? Nah. These are the Boggs boys. Lifelong ne'er-do-wells. You're lucky they didn't just set your house afire. I believe these two have spent more time behind bars than they've been free men."

Back inside, Kathy said, "I love you, Rick. But sometimes ... I don't know. Shooting out the doors? I suppose I should be used to this kind of stuff by now." She gave a head shake like the one she delivered when she'd come up from the garage.

"Hey. That guy was going to shoot Audrey. He had his gun aimed. I could have shot him I suppose, but that seemed like a bit much."

She poured herself a glass of wine and went outside. It seemed a bit early but I had an adrenaline buzz myself and was glad I wasn't any place where my having a drink would be acceptable behavior. Besides, Kathy's white wine was the only alcoholic beverage in the house, something no self-respecting serious drinker would imbibe until they got drunk on something more substantial and there was nothing else around. A tonic and lime would have to do for now.

Joining her, I sat for a few minutes while we filled the air with silence. Finally, I got antsy enough to say, "What did you think was going to happen here? Did you think I was just going to have a chat with those boys, tell them we didn't like what they were doing and please don't do it again?"

"The problem was," she began, "I hadn't thought it through. I think I was as much caught up in the drama of the thing as you were. Okay, we're gonna play a trick on these guys. That's as far as I got. I was really excited when I saw them at the community center. I just wish—and I know this isn't going to happen—that you didn't have a gun."

"You have a gun, too," I said, referring to the revolver she had in the night stand next to our bed.

She looked at me with a witchy grin and said, "Yes, I do."

"Oh, jeez. Maybe I shouldn't have reminded you."

She leaned over the table and wiggled her finger, calling me over. We kissed. We both sighed, as if we'd each been holding our breath for a long time.

"I'm gonna call Detective Fair," I said after we regained composure. "I want to go down and sign my statement about the break-in when he's there, fill him in on what's been going on."

"On what he doesn't already know, you mean," Kathy said. "Before you go, explain to me about the Calhouns again. I'm still not clear as to why they want us off the case."

"One scenario is that they murdered Revis. Maybe they have the money, maybe they don't, but they don't want us poking around. And their involvement in it might explain why the sheriff is disinclined to conduct more of an investigation."

"Good ole boys' network," Kathy said. "But didn't I recently hear you say you thought this current sheriff is a good guy."

"Yeah. I think he is. But I want to keep the idea on the table. The Calhouns could be responsible for Revis's death, and could be the sheriff's department isn't more aggressive about pursuing the murder possibilities for reasons having nothing to do with corruption."

"Maybe the Calhouns don't have the money but are trying to find it."

"Right. And if we, Peters and Ryder Investigators, are as good as they think we are, we just might find it first."

"How would they know about the existence of the loot?"

"Ah. Spoken like a hard-boiled dick. I think if that much money were in the area looking for a place to land, people like the Calhouns would hear about it."

"What about this?" she offered. "The sheriff also thinks the Calhouns are looking for the money and they're keeping an eye on them."

"Follow the Calhouns, find the cash?"

"It could be another explanation for why the sheriff is not, apparently, aggressively pursuing this case. Maybe they really are and we don't know it. They aren't—not even your friend Detective Fair—going to tell you everything they're doing."

"As he reminds me."

***

While walking up to the building where I would give my written statement about the morning's events and meet with Detective Fair, I saw the Boggs boys coming out of the County Detention Center, aka, the jailhouse. I was not surprised.

Fair was on his phone but at my knock he signaled me in. After hanging up, he said, "I heard you met a couple of the county's more colorful denizens today."

"I did," I said as I sat in the chair next to his desk. "But meeting them was only one of the highlights of the day."

"Oh?"

"Also of interest was learning that they work for the Calhouns, a tribe of which we'd never heard until these lads started coming around."

"Well, now. That is something. How did you connect them?"

"Traced their license plates. You know, Detective— detective work." Fair appeared unamused. I continued. "The way we put things together, we surmise that the Calhouns are in the marijuana production business."

"So I've heard. And don't get all up in your stuff about that, thinking, if we know about them, how come they're still in business? You are not that naïve. And you know, if it wasn't them, it would be somebody else out there doin' it. At least these are local boys and relatively benign."

"Dealing with the devil you know, you mean?"

"Something like that."

"Another interesting occurrence was seeing the Boggs boys walk out of jail a few minutes ago. There was hardly time for them to be arraigned. Must have good counsel." The detective remained sphinx-like. "And I presume the car I saw them get into is owned by JS Enterprises, the folks who own the pickup truck those boys run around in."

"Reasonable presumption."

We gazed across the table at each other as if waiting for the other to draw. He blinked.

"Got anything else for me?"

"'Fraid not. Kathy and I were commiserating about how our suspect list keeps growing. I'm becoming more sympathetic with the county's decision to name it suicide and call it a day."

"Self-inflicted, intentional or otherwise."

"Yeah. Could have been an accident. That's right."

"I hear attitude in your voice, Ryder."

"Oh? Imagine that." I raised my hand as if to say, I surrender. "I realize we're coming at this from different angles. And that's not going to change for you unless something, a smoking-gun kind of thing, comes to you that changes your mind. And we—that would be Kathy and I—are coming at it from the assumption that we will find that smoking gun."

Fair looked across his desk at me with an uninformative expression. "At what point do you decide there isn't one?"

This was an excellent question. With so many suspects we pushed right on, possibly in arrogance, ignoring the possibility that the law enforcement people had it right all along: self-inflicted overdose, intentional or unintentional.

"I'm not sure," I acknowledged.

He nodded, having perfected the noncommittal cop nod. "Makes it hard to know when you're approaching the end of the road if there's no sign saying, 'end of the road'."

"I guess that's how we'll know if there's nothing more to be discovered. When the road ceases to go anywhere."

"This metaphorical stuff makes my head hurt. So, you will

let me know, in the absence of a smoking gun, when you've run out of road."

"You'll be the first to know. Maybe the second, after our client."

He smiled as he said, "The ever-delightful and engaging Ms. Queenie Weaver."

"That would be her."

"I doubt if she remembers me, but back in the mid-eighties, I guess I was about fifteen, the cops, the PO-lice in the vernacular—although my mother would have smacked my mouth if she heard me say it—had done something egregiously wrong to a person of color and we were marchin' around the cop stand, wavin' signs, chanting, yelling, the whole nine yards. I was particularly full of my righteous self. Queenie was there, as she was at most civil rights-related action back then. This was thirty-some years ago. Asheville was not what you would call a paragon of integration. Nor, sadly, is it today but that's another matter. Anyway, Queenie came up to me and suggested, in that fine mountain drawl of hers, that I might want to tune it down, that the point of what we were doing was not to get more black people arrested. She suggested that neither of my parents would look kindly on the prospect of having to come downtown to bail my sorry ass out of jail. I remember being particularly taken by her use of that phrase, 'sorry ass.' Nice lookin' white lady talkin' street. I liked her."

"I take it you didn't have to go to jail."

"No. My folks didn't think corporal punishment was a very enlightened manner of parenting, but I knew that getting arrested would have earned me a whuppin'."

"I'll tell her you say, 'Hey,' next time I see her."

***

Y ou still think a trip to Chapel Hill might be productive?"
I asked while we were breakfasting on bacon and eggs
along with some pastries I'd picked up downtown.

"Who knows? I'm sure it would annoy Dr. Philips if
he knew we were there checking up on him. Maybe we can
accomplish the same thing with the phone and internet. That's
how it's supposed to be these days, isn't it?"

"Tell me again why it was you flew out to Colorado."

"Oh. Yes. The idea of face-to-face contact. There is that. I
guess I could get on the phone and start checking around, see
who we 'd want to talk to if we got the chance."

"The more I think about it, the more I like the Philips-
Ballard scenario," I said. "Both of them seething with
resentment of Revis who has set himself up as a guru, the
authority on the state of medical marijuana research and, like
some academic black hole, sucking up as much credit as he can
for himself."

"'Seething'?"

"Dramatic license."

As Kathy got up with the plates, Audrey stood as if some
invisible drill instructor had yelled, "Fall in," and followed her
to the kitchen. He was rewarded with scraps of scones and egg.
To judge from the workings of his tail, he couldn't believe his
luck. I prepared coffee refills.

"Think Philips might be recruiting her to go to Carolina
and work with him?" Kathy speculated.

"Never occurred to me. Doesn't seem too far-fetched.
Would be nice if we had a contact down there."

For a few minutes the only sounds were of the creek
tumbling over itself alongside the house, birds chattering,
summer insects chirping. It was so serene even the cats felt
comfortable keeping company with us. We agreed that, as

much as it would be nice to spend the whole day right there, we did have work to do.

The landline rang as we approached the upstairs office. Kathy took it. I gleaned from her end of the conversation that it had something to do with a presumed disloyal mate.

"Woman thinks her partner is cheating on her," she reported after hanging up.

"Peters and Ryder on the case," I crowed.

"Could be interesting. Her partner is a woman."

I thought for a moment. "Is this the first case of suspected same-sex infidelity we've worked, Dr. Watson?"

"I believe it is, Holmes."

"I'll let you have this one," I said.

"You'll let me have this one? Since when do you get to decide who gets what?"

"Oops. Lost my head there. Sorry. Let me rephrase that."

"Please."

"Honey? I was wondering if you'd like to take the lead on this case?"

"Really! Gosh. That would be terrific."

"Someday we'll have to get the neighbors over to referee a sarcasm match."

"So, what about Chapel Hill?" she asked. "I guess you'll have to do that."

"We're back to figuring out how we get in down there without ruffling Philips's feathers."

"Without further ruffling Philips's feathers," she offered.

"Without further flustering Philips's feathers," I countered.

"Enough. Enough. Yes. Is that something you will put your wits to—if you haven't just used up your supply for the month—so I can get on with the Case of the Stepping Out Sapphist."

"Okay. I'll give up the alliterative affectations if you will."

"Deal. And you're taking over the Philips phase of the investigation?"

"Stop it! Jeez. Yes. I will pursue—"

"Don't even go there," she warned.

"I was merely going to say I will pursue, okay, strike that. I will follow up with possibilities at UNC. To that end, I think I'll take Audrey for a walk up the road, see if anything shakes loose."

"You boys have a good time."

The air was warm, eighty degrees, perhaps, but there was something in it, a hint that cooler days were coming. Great white puff balls slid gracefully on the blue sea above us. The wind whispering in the pines was barely audible. Audrey ran in serpentine fashion like someone trying to avoid being shot. I knew that at each change of direction a new smell had distracted him from his previous goal, kind of like my mind was doing as I leaped from one scenario to the next. I was covering great distance without getting anywhere. By the time we returned to the house I'd concluded that the best course of action was a web search of Philips's peers, much as we'd done with the faculty at East Colorado State.

As the hound and I were walking up the drive, Kathy was exiting the garage.

"Going to meet Ramona for coffee," she called out the window. "Be back in an hour or so. In time for lunch, anyway. I think this'll be interesting."

"When was the last case we had that wasn't?"

"Interesting in a different kind of way."

"You're not thinking of going over to the other side, are you?"

"You are a real jerk sometimes, you know?" As she was backing away, she called out, "But I love you anyway!"

Nothing of note jumped out at me as I pored over the endless Chapel Hill faculty web pages. Part of the craft of this work is to be able to cope with the strain of going down a path with nothing to show for it long enough that something eventually comes out of the woods. This is based on the notion that what you are looking for is there to be found. In the Case of the Untimely Demise of Professor Revis, others were not as sure as we were that what we were seeking—evidence that he died from the nefarious actions of others—existed.

My concentration was fading and I turned my attention to the detritus collecting on my desk where I spotted the pictures of the 1991 Jaguar XJS I had printed off the computer. Following my sleuth's code of not looking for anything in particular, I was simply looking to see if anything caught my eye. After shuffling the pages a couple of time, something did.

I left a message on Art Revis's cellphone asking him to call me at his convenience. His work phone advised me that he would be gone until next Wednesday. I left a similar message there, hoping that he was checking calls on one or the other of the machines sooner than four days hence.

I got up and paced the room, knowing that this could be a dead end but juiced with the possibility that it might be a bona fide breakthrough. There being nothing to do about it at the moment, I resumed my exploration of UNC faculty.

A paper by Dr. Philips and two people at the University

of West Oregon got my attention. It was highly technical, as one would expect, dealing with a particular cannabinoid of marijuana which might have a specific medical use, exactly the kind of work Revis was doing. A conversation with one of those Oregon scientists could be enlightening. Before I had gotten to follow up with that thought, I realized I was famished.

Kathy surfaced from the garage as I arrived in the kitchen. We threw a large Greek salad together and took it outside.

"How'd it go?" I asked, sitting on my excitement.

"Good. Ramona's a charming woman. Fiftiesh. Quite pretty. Platinum hair in a pixie cut. An attractive package altogether. She and her partner—Alyson, with a y—have been in a relationship for fifteen years but over the past year Ramona feels they've grown apart. Recently, Alyson's been gone for unexplained reasons. Late coming home from work. Going out to do errands on the weekends for long periods of time. That kind of thing. Alyson denies that anything is amiss. Ramona wants to know what's going on."

"Sounds like standard stuff."

"I'll do some tailing. Want to join me on stake-outs?"

"First let me tell you what's going on with Revis."

Upstairs in the office, I showed her pictures of the Jaguar and told her what I suspected.

"Even if you're right," she said after hearing what I was thinking, "we still won't know who the guilty party is."

"No. But it would be evidence that something happened up there of which the police are either ignorant or are ignoring. There's more than simply a dead body."

"And you can't talk to Art until Wednesday?"

"If he gets one of my messages, it could be sooner."

"Could his wife help you get in touch with him?"

"Maybe if I had a phone number other than the home landline which gives the standard, 'Please leave a message' message."

"You could drive up there on the chance she'd be around."

"Long drive on speculation. In the meantime, there's the UNC work."

"Oh, my gosh. I almost forgot. Do you remember my cousin Emily's daughter, Melody?"

"The one whose wedding we went to last year?"

"That's the one. On my way home it dawned on me that she's at Chapel Hill now. I think she teaches botany, and if she does, she probably knows Philips—or at least would know of him. She might have some suggestions about who to talk to."

"Alright! Giver 'er a call." I loved it when things like this came together. Serendipity. Some people think there are forces in the universe responsible for such fortuitous alignments. The idea that "there are no coincidences." I'm more inclined to accept the randomness of the universe. Stuff just happens.

Kathy left a message at Melody's university number.

"What did we do before we left messages for people?" she mused.

"That's kind of like 'what did we do before telephones?' There've been answering machines around as long as I can remember. Before that, you just had to keep calling. And before that you sent letters and went to see people. I'm not sure the new technology is an improvement."

"C'mon, Rick," she said. "Was going to the moon a good idea? Sending people out in space? Can't have one without the other."

"Can't have space exploration without voice mail?"

"Technological innovation. If you open the box you have

no idea what'll come out."

"Okay, okay. I'll take the voice mail. I still think we've lost something."

"Of course we have," she said. "Just like we lost the leisurely ways of getting around when the horseless carriage arrived."

I had to decide if I was going to continue my research into the UNC faculty or wait to hear from Melody who might have information which would render my work superfluous. Fortunately, I didn't have to wait long. From what I could hear of the conversation, Melody had information that could be useful. A trip to Chapel Hill was mentioned.

"Tomorrow lunch?" Kathy responded, looking over at me. I nodded.

Kathy said, "Yes," then laughed and said, "Oh, yes."

After hanging up, she was still chuckling. "Apparently there's a place in Chapel Hill known far and wide for its BLT sandwiches loaded with bacon and she wanted to be sure you liked bacon, although there are other ... "

I raised my hand. "Enough. I'm in with bacon."

Ten

Saturday

I don't mind driving by myself and often prefer it. But the journey east on I-40 through the foothills and into the Piedmont was so familiar I could almost do it in my sleep. Music is de rigeur. Rock 'n roll. Springsteen. Old Jimi Hendrix. Live at Woodstock. People I'd grown up with. Mixed with sufficient caffeine, the trip breezed by.

Melody was standing outside the front door of the restaurant and called out "Uncle Rick!" as I walked up. I'm not sure I would have recognized her. The wedding was the only occasion when we'd been in the same vicinity but, as I am continually reminded, I'm hard to miss. After a genial hug, she said, "Aunt Kathy said you like bacon. I hope she was right because they have the most ridiculously terrific BLT here. Actually, it's more of a BBBLT."

"All the way here I've been telling my arteries to get ready for the onslaught."

After we'd been seated, she said, "Aunt Kathy said you were interested in information about the Biology Department faculty?"

"I'm actually not sure it's biology or something else. And would you mind dropping the 'Aunt' and 'Uncle'? I know it's meant to be affectionate and proper but it sounds weird. Rick and Kathy will do, if that's okay."

"Sure. To tell you the truth, I didn't know what to call you."

"I'd like to be able to talk to some people about Randall Philips without him knowing about it."

Her eyebrows flared. "Ooh. Dr. Philips. Sounds intriguing."

"It is. And at some point I hope to tell you all about it."

"But now's not the time."

"Unfortunately."

"And you want dirt on him."

"Well, maybe not dirt, but … well, all right, yes. Dirt. We're looking into the circumstances of the death of Dr. Marc Revis."

"I heard about that. He committed suicide or something?"

"It's the 'or something' that Kathy and I are looking into. Dr. Revis was in Asheville for a conference about the medical uses of marijuana. It had been organized by Dr. Philips."

Her jaw dropped. She looked like a Southern Baptist who'd been told that Billy Graham admitted to being gay. She leaned toward me. "You think Dr. Philips had something to do with Dr. Revis's death?"

"We understand there was significant professional jealousy between the men. That's why we want to talk to someone who knows Philips but doesn't have a stake in his research."

"But he's such a kind of—" She looked around as if to make sure no one could hear her. "Doofus. You know?"

"The epitome of your college professor?"

She grinned. "So what am I?"

"Not the epitome of your college professor. But Philips is the kind of guy you can't image doing something like that, right?"

"Absolutely."

"And so, we're back to, is there anyone you know who might be willing to talk to me about Dr. Philips and his relationship with Dr. Revis?"

"There is a woman ... "

Our sandwiches arrived and the BBBLT was as terrific as advertised. Fresh tomatoes, crisp lettuce, the right amount of mayo, and bacon, bacon, bacon. The restaurant owners must have had an interest in a hog farm or a cardiology practice.

When we'd finished lunch, acknowledging to each other that dessert at that point would be gilding the lily, I thanked Melody for her information. We exchanged "hope to see you again" sentiments, both knowing it was unlikely to happen any time soon.

I left a phone message with the woman whom Melody suggested might have some interesting gossip, if not hard data, about Dr. Philips. While waiting for a call back, I strolled the main street of the college town. Although it had changed considerably since my last visit here, in many ways it remained the same. Paralleling the university, the street had managed to maintain its college town feel. I was headed to the arboretum on campus when Maria Gutierrez's return call came. She agreed to meet with me over coffee at 4:30 that afternoon.

The toll of driving from Asheville plus the excessive consumption of pig fat rendered me lethargic. After a brief stroll among the garden's paths, I took a seat on an old bench overlooking a pond. A half-hour later I woke up, remembering I had a meter to feed. The coffee shop where my meeting with Maria was to take place was a few blocks from the car.

I bought a latte and settled in at the counter overlooking the street, much like I did at my favorite bookstore in Asheville. According to the university's website, Ms. Gutierrez had been on the faculty of the Joint Department of Biomedical

Engineering for three years, which would have brought her in direct contact with Philips. I restrained from pumping my fist in the air.

At 4:30 there was a tap on my shoulder. I turned to see a raven-haired beauty smiling at me. I was smitten and knew that Kathy would understand.

"Mr. Ryder," she said, an observation not a question.

"How did you guess, Ms. Gutierrez? And 'Rick' will do."

"And Maria for me. Shall we find a table? Toward the back I think would be good." Her 'r's had a slight trill to them, adding to her charm.

I let her lead the way to a table for two situated in a far corner. She sat with her back to the room.

"I've spoken to Melody since our conversation so I have some idea what you're interested in, but she didn't go into detail about why you're interested."

"I presume you know that Professor Philips organized a medical marijuana conference in Asheville which took place a couple of weeks ago." She nodded. "Dr. Marc Revis from East Colorado University was scheduled to be the keynote speaker. The day he was to speak, his body was found near a cabin where he had been staying outside of Asheville. I've had two conversations with Randy since then, hoping he might know something that would help in finding out who killed the professor. Our discussions have not been fruitful."

"Aren't the police investigating this?"

"Good question. The police have decided that the cause of death was an overdose of alcohol and a prescription sleeping pill. And, while there's no controversy about that, some of us are not convinced that he took those substances of his own volition."

"I'm not sure what you mean."

"My wife and I—we're partners in a private investigation business—we believe that someone doctored his drink or drinks. We also believe that Revis was traveling with a very large sum of money. One scenario is that he was intentionally given enough drugs to kill him so that someone could take that money. Alternately, someone may have misjudged the dose, perhaps hoping to render him unconscious rather than killing him, and stealing the money while he was out of it."

"If it was the latter, wouldn't there have been the risk that Dr. Revis would know who it was if he regained consciousness?"

"Good point. But we know that he'd been drinking and smoking pot before he got to the cabin that night. If the culprits assumed he'd wake up at some point, they may have been counting on him having no recollection of who'd been in the cabin with him."

She smiled and nodded, then asked, "Are you in a hurry to get back to Asheville?"

"Not particularly. Why do you ask?"

"I thought a walk in the botanical gardens might be nice. They aren't far."

"Yes, I know. I just came from there."

"It might be more conducive to a candid conversation."

On our way out of the restaurant, it was hard to tell on which one of us garnered the most attention, the one-armed man or the dazzling woman.

On the walk, she asked what had happened to my arm. I gave her the short-form response. Automobile accident at age 18, leaving out the part about the accompanying death.

We found a bench off the beaten path. The wind had shifted, bringing drier, cooler air. I could have stayed there for hours even by myself.

"Dr. Philips is a very smart guy," she said, "maybe genius.

Unfortunately, he has lousy leadership skills. His program is floundering and he was—is—under pressure to achieve results. I wasn't involved in the conference planning, but as I understand it, he was hoping it would help get his program back on the map. As much as he doesn't care for Marc Revis, he felt he had to have him to be the keynote speaker."

"Were their programs in competition?"

"You mean for grants, like that? I suppose so. Marc Revis had a reputation as a good salesman. Something that can't be said for Dr. Philips."

"Have you heard that the money Revis brought with him was for the purpose of buying land for marijuana production?"

"The story about the money is in the air over in the department. Not everyone is talking about it, but everybody seems to know about it."

"And is everyone aware that Dr. Revis drove out to Asheville with a young woman?"

"This is the first I've heard that."

"She wound up giving the keynote address. With the support of Dr. Philips."

"Really?"

"Really. And presumably she knew about the money, too."

Maria appeared to be genuinely surprised. And intrigued.

"You don't think that they ... ?" She stopped mid-question.

"That they killed Dr. Revis?" I filled in.

She shrugged and grimaced. "Wow."

"Knowing Dr. Philips as you do, does it seem within the realm of possibilities that he would be involved in a killing? Maybe he didn't do it. But perhaps colluded with whoever did."

"Philips? Hard to imagine. But isn't that what people say all the time? He just didn't seem the type?"

"That seems to be how the most unlikely people can get

away with the most outrageous things. I also wonder about his drinking. Is there any talk about that?"

She stood up and stretched, took a few steps, looked around. "It seems that people will talk about almost anything—sexual infidelity, money issues, whatever—but when it comes to drinking ... Maybe it's because so many of us do it and have mixed feelings about it for ourselves. But, yes, I have seen him over-imbibe on more than one occasion."

"So, maybe while he was drinking he got talked into doing away with his nemesis."

"This sounds like an episode of a TV show, you know that one with that old lady up in New England?"

"Except this is not a TV show," I said. "A real flesh-and-blood person has died. And I think it's likely it was at the hands of others."

Her expression changed. We weren't talking about some anonymous death. This was about a death that might involve a colleague.

"I'm sorry. I didn't mean to make light of Dr. Revis's ... passing."

"Let's walk. You seem antsy and I've been on my butt most of the day. "

When we were both on our feet, I asked, "Can you think of anyone else around the university who might have been interested in seeing Marc Revis dead? Maybe someone who knew about the money and could have been in cahoots with Philips?"

"That sounds so cold."

"Murder is pretty much that."

She shivered. "I know. It's something I've never dealt with before."

"Most people haven't. Thank goodness most of us follow

the ninth commandment, whether we're religious or not."

"I don't know much about other peoples' relationships with Dr. Philips, but I can't imagine any of them would even think of murder."

"Sure they would. Everybody thinks of murder. That's why the ninth commandment reminds us not to do it."

"I don't think about murdering anybody," she said.

"Sure you do. Some old boyfriend, girlfriend, the jerk who cut you off in traffic. Tell me you've never even thought about it."

After a moment she said, "Okay. I get it. But I can't think of anyone who would have had reason to kill Dr. Revis."

"From what you know about Philips, do you think he'd want Revis out of the way?"

"Again, I'm not really that close—"

"I understand that. But from what you do know."

"I can't answer that."

The warmth had gone out of her voice and her posture was more rigid. I was afraid I might have alienated her.

"I sense we've gone down this road as far as is productive. I'll stop now except to say, if you think of anything that might remotely relate to all this, I'd appreciate it if you let me know."

Her face lightened; her body relaxed. She might yet have something for the team.

Back at the entrance to the arboretum, I asked if she needed a lift somewhere.

"I hadn't thought about you driving," she said. "That must be interesting."

"Modern technology is great. I'm probably less of risk on the highway than ninety-five percent of the two-handed drivers out there."

She declined the ride but agreed to get in touch with me if

something came to mind or if she heard anything that might be of interest to me. After we shook hands, I instructed myself to not to stare as she walked away.

Fatigue seeped into my bones as I contemplated the drive back to the mountains. The thought of another doze in the gardens came to me and was superseded by the idea of more caffeine. The meter had run out on my car and I fed it only enough to allow me to cross the street and grab an iced double latte to go. I called Kathy when I got to the car.

"The sense I get is that, although no one thinks of Philips as a killer, there would be those who wouldn't be surprised if he were somehow involved."

"Nothing like, 'Dr. Philips? Sure he'd murder Marc Revis in a New York minute'?"

"Afraid not."

"Have you heard back from Art?"

I'd almost forgotten I was expecting his call. "No. Maybe it's time to try again. I'd rather not have to make another trip up there. What's happening with Ramona?"

"It turns out her partner went exactly where she said she was going and did exactly what she said she was going to do. I told Ramona that there might be something else going on in their relationship other that one of them having an affair and that I couldn't help with that. Gee whiz, Rick. Where are all the juicy cases? People sneaking in and out of hotel rooms, that kind of thing. You've had them. How come I don't get any?"

"Didn't you just have one of those?"

"Yeah. But that was all innocent."

"It's your spirit, dear. Your 'chi' as Anne McDonald would say. You're such a sweet, loving person that your consciousness will simply not allow any tawdry mess to come into it."

Silence. Five seconds. "I know all the good herb is supposed to be up here," she said, "but did one of those co-eds you met with get you high?"

"No. And you and I have been on some pretty interesting—and tawdry—cases together."

"We have. But I want my own."

"Okay, Nora Charles, we'll see what we can do to increase your exposure to the seamy side of life."

Another phone call to Art got the same response as my previous calls and I seriously considering driving up there in the hopes that he or that his wife might be around. The trip would take a little over three hours. I could spend the night or drive back home in the dark. I'd have to decide by the time I got to Statesville, where I-77 crosses I-40, whether to go home or head north.

Ten minutes later, he saved me from doing anything drastic.

"Sorry it's taken so long to get back to you. But I was at a conference in Chapel Hill."

When I started laughing, he asked, "What's so funny about that?"

He laughed as well when I told him where I'd spent the day.

"But, you wouldn't have been able to do what I'm going to ask you for until you got home, anyway."

"And what's would that be?"

When I told him, he said, "Well, that's easy enough, if a little strange."

"I know. And when this is all done, I'll let you know why I wanted it."

Within ten minutes the photos I'd asked him for appeared on my cell phone.

The hit of caffeine kept my mind buzzing. I had a lot invested in the Philips-Ballard scenario. It would have helped to know where Cheri had spent the nights before and after Revis died. I wondered if there were a way to get my hands on the hotel log to see if she'd checked into a room for herself. That wouldn't negate the possibility that she paid for a room and didn't use it. Still, it could be useful to find out if she was sharing a room or to contact those in rooms next to her, a very labor-intensive activity. All the more reason why Peters and Ryder Investigations needed an intern.

Queenie was receding in my mind as an active suspect. If there were, indeed, a gray van involved, that would help remove her from my list altogether. The way Art responded to my request tended to exonerate him, too, at least to me. Which could have been exactly why he had been so cooperative. If I was wandering along the right path, that left the Calhouns and Anne McDonald along with the Philips-Ballard cabal.

Given that Anne and her ex had resumed communication, she probably knew he was coming to the conference as well as where he would be staying, very likely knew of his sleeping pills use and even, perhaps, the whereabouts of the money. A scene developed in the theater of my mind.

She is at the cabin when he returns from the conference. Suggests a drink; she would have brought the booze along with her and prepared it with the pills. He drinks and passes out.

As the scene closes, I wonder if she would have been able to get her ex-husband into the outbuilding. Perhaps he did wander there of his own volition. Maybe it made no difference where he passed out and died. As I had thought before, maybe killing him wasn't the objective. Simply getting him out of the way until the money was recovered might have been enough.

I'd made up a scenario where Revis wouldn't remember

what had happened if he regained consciousness. Or, if he had wakened up and seemed to remember, he could be persuaded his memory was wrong. I couldn't think of an easy way to rule Anne in or out. I assumed that she, like Queenie, would not have been driving a gray van. On the other hand, the gray van may have nothing to do with any of this, a red herring of my own creation.

By the time I got to Winston-Salem, both the Honda and my body needed rejuvenation. After satisfying the needs of the car, I found a hole-in-the-wall Thai place on the outskirts of a mega-shopping center. With more coffee from a nearby café, I was ready for the last two-hour leg of the journey.

As I approached Hickory, with the ridges of the southern Appalachians visible against the setting sun, another possibility revealed itself.

Eleven

Sunday

Kathy squeezed oranges while I whipped up pancake batter. Bacon sizzled on a nearby burner as I dropped dollops of better onto a hot griddle. Ten minutes later we were outside along with the hound. The cats kept guard at the corners of the deck while we brunched and read the papers, having agreed we would avoid work until the Sunday morning ritual was complete.

With the plates cleared and the kitchen in order, we reviewed *The Case of Doctor Revis's Untimely Demise*. Kathy agreed that we could dismiss Queenie from further consideration and that the Ballard-Philips cabal was a promising possibility.

"What about Anne McDonald?" she asked.

"Funny you ask." I explained the revelation I'd had in the car on the way home.

"You're kidding."

I shrugged. "No. Not kidding. I'm not sure it's a realistic scenario, but I wasn't kidding."

"That's.... I don't know. It sounds like something that would happen on one of those afternoon soap operas."

"I wonder how long the conference had been scheduled before it took place," I said. "Seems like it was a pretty big thing."

"You think she moved back to this area because she knew he'd be here for the conference and would be bringing all that cash with him?"

I pondered that while I refilled our respective cups of tea and coffee, realizing I didn't have a good answer for that. After a first sip of her tea she went on, "You think Art was a party to this?"

"Merely speculating. I know, it seems like a long shot."

Kathy put on her I-can-see-it-in-my-mind look and her voice took on the smooth, hypnotic—and very sexy—quality she uses when she stops hypothesizing and starts imagining.

"She and Art drive down together in her car and are at the cabin before Marc returns from his day at the conference. They bring along a bottle of bourbon, not knowing that he'd already had a couple of drinks, but knowing it was his drink of choice. They also have some pot. For a while they sit around, make small talk, smoke the pot, drink the bourbon. But his drinks have been doped—the same scenario that we've laid out for our other suspects. He passes out. They carry him to the barn and lay him out. Anne checks the house while Marc's examining the car. Being the mechanical engineering type he is, he can tell if and where large amount of bills would be hidden. They find the loot, Art drives away in the Jag, while Mom heads home in her car."

"Diabolical," I said. "I'm impressed you could think that way."

"Aw, shucks. You say the nicest things."

"Problem is, he didn't take the car away until the next day."

"How do we know this?"

"From Queenie. Remember? I got all over her for not telling us Art had come to get it?"

"Now I do. That doesn't mean they couldn't have been

here that night, done what they came to do and gone home. Marc comes down the next day to make it seem like he'd been out of town the night before."

"You said, 'gone home.' Home to where? Celo? Blacksburg?"

Irritation crept into her voice. "How would I know?"

"That was actually a rhetorical question. And I don't think I've asked either of those two where they were that night."

"Why not?"

"Don't know. Sounds too much like a cop. I mean, nobody's required to tell us anything."

"I'll leave that interrogation to you," she said. "For the sake of discussion, how do you think the idea of Art and Anne stacks up against a scenario involving the Calhouns and the two stooges?"

I felt like I was thinking out loud. "Anne and Art's goal is more immediate. Get the money. They have no dog in the who-grows-marijuana fight. My guess is that if, indeed, they were the perpetrators, Revis's death was accidental. What would he have done if he had awakened the next day and found the money missing? Go to the police? Where's his evidence that he ever had the money? And when he accuses his ex-wife and son of stealing it, they merely say, 'We have no idea what you're talking about.' Oh. There is one other thing. I'm not sure how this fits. I asked Art to send me some photos of the Jaguar, which he did."

I explained exactly what he'd sent.

"And you think that's some kind of relevant evidence?"

"I think it suggests there is, in fact, a smoking gun."

"And you think he has it?"

"Or someone beat him to it."

"Okay Mr. Hotshot Investigator, what do we do next?"

"Talk to our client."

"Oh, yeah. I'd almost forgotten. This is business, not an entertainment."

The tips of the pine trees had turned bronze; red tinged the edges of the dogwoods. Sonny came down to shepherd us up the approach to the house. Queenie was on the porch in a rocker. Rather than greeting us at the head of the stairs, she waited for us to approach before she rose.

"What a delight," she said after giving hugs all around. "Sit. I'll bring tea."

"I'll join you," Kathy offered.

After the women disappeared into the house, I soaked in the mountain splendor. My mind slipped into a fantasy about Queenie winding up with the missing money and being able to buy back some of the land around her that had been sold off by previous Weaver generations.

Soon there were chocolate chip cookies, not the kind you get from the store, and the requisite iced tea on the porch table.

"So, what's the big news that has y'all comin' out here?"

"You don't think we came out simply to enjoy your company?"

She gave me a gimme a break look, eyes narrowed, chin dropped.

"See," I began, "that's one of the benefits of having you as a client. We get to visit with you as part of the business."

"Stow it, Ryder. What's goin' on?"

"The truth is," Kathy said, "we're kind of stuck. It's no wonder the cops decided Marc's death was self-inflicted. It saved a lot of work. The two scenarios we like best are a Dr. Philips-Cheri Ballard connection, and a joint Art Revis and Anne McDonald venture."

"Anne? Marc's ex-wife?"

"The one," Kathy said.

"And their son, Art?" Her voice was filled with wonder.

"That's one of the possibilities we're considering. And then there are the Calhouns."

"The Calhouns? You haven't told me about them."

"We've been busy," I said, more defensively than necessary.

"Of course it would be them," Queenie pronounced. "Jeez. I don't know why I didn't think of them. Keep other people from buyin' up the land and pocketing the better part of a million dollars in the process. That's it. So, what's the problem?"

"How would they do it? How would they get Marc to drink the drugged bourbon? And how would they know where the money was?"

"I didn't think anybody knew where the money was," Queenie said. "I thought that was the point of getting him to pass out, so that the perpetrators would have time to search for it."

Something, that intuitive sleuth sense, kept me from saying I don't think a search would turn it up. Kathy didn't realize it but we had begun to play poker and I didn't want to show my hand, even to our client and friend. Instead, I said, "That's been our assumption up until now. But I'm beginning to question it."

"Meaning," Queenie said, "that you think whoever did this—killed Marc—knew where the money was."

"That's what I'm beginning to think."

"Kathy?" our hostess asked.

"I'm with my partner."

"And?"

"And, we're not sure what that means," I said.

"I have a feeling you're getting closer, in spite of what you said earlier, and that you're not going to share all you know with me."

"Queenie," I said, "it's not easy to put something past you."

"Shit, Ryder. Don't go blowin' smoke up my butt. Don't feel good at this time of my life. But I understand why you might want to keep somethings to yourselves. You're the pros. You do this the way you think is best."

Queenie leaned back in her rocker. She seemed tired.

"Anything we can do for you while we're here?" Kathy asked.

"Like?"

"Oh, I don't know. Fix a meal for you…?

"Kathy Peters," the older woman said. "I may run out of gas more quickly than I used to but I can still take care of myself. What's the term? The Activities of Daily Living? I'm not ready for home health yet."

"I'm sorry, Queenie. Really. I—"

"It's okay, dear. I love the both of you. But I do hope you can wrap this thing up soon. It weighs heavy on me. Marc had been a good friend. Like all of us, he'd changed over the years, but I still thought he was a decent human being and he didn't deserve to be killed."

As we drove down the other side of the mountain and passed the cabin, I thought about going in just for the heck of it, see if anything previously hidden from view would reveal itself. Kathy encouraged me to leave it alone. We went on down to the Pressley place. SaraJean was out on the small garden patio at the side of the house as we pulled into the drive, legs up on a lounge chair, sipping a beer.

"Stay put," Kathy said. "You look too comfortable to move."

"Hello, you two. Pull up some chairs. Get you something to drink?"

We declined, Kathy saying, "Just had tea with Queenie."

"How is the old bird today?"

"She seemed tired," Kathy said. "She okay?"

"I don't rightly know. She sure doesn't have the stamina she used to. And she's not all that old, you know? Seventy-four, I think. It's like something just came over her."

"What are the chances she'll go see a doctor?" I asked.

"Slim to none."

"And how are you two?" I ventured.

"I'm okay if I can stay away from him for a few hours a day." She tilted her head toward the house. "Sometimes he finds my last nerve and pounces on it."

"Still can't get him out of the house?" Kathy asked.

"He is such a stick-in-mud. You'd think he'd get tired sittin' 'round all day, getting' high, watchin' stupid TV. I really think his main entertainment is buggin' the hell out of me." Then, as if someone had switched channels, her face brightened. "Come on in. Say 'hi' to the old fart. I've got somethin' I'm workin' on to show you."

Inside, an old Dick Van Dyke Show rerun played on the television. Arlo had dozed off.

"He'll come around in a minute. Here. I want you to see these."

 Pictures of vans were laid out on the coffee table.

"See this one?" she asked pointing to a cut-away view showing the interior of what otherwise looked like a standard, full-sized van. It showed a wheelchair where the driver's seat would ordinarily be and a captain's chair in the passenger place. "He could motor his wheelchair right up the back end of it, right into the driver's place. Look. There are all the controls, right on the steering wheel."

"A little like my car," I said.

"Yeah. Hadn't thought of that. Yeah. It's sure somethin' what they can do these days. See, then he wouldn't have to rely on me. He could go anywhere he wanted, whenever he wanted."

"She'll do about anything to get me away from here," came a voice from behind us. "Away from her, actually."

"Arlo," I said, "nice to see you're not gonna sleep through our entire visit."

"I heard you come in. Waitin' for an auspicious moment to make my presence known."

"What do you think about the stuff SaraJean's been showing us?"

"I dunno. I know I should get out of this place now and then. I'm sure I've killed off a zillion brain cells just settin' around."

"That pot ain't helpin' 'em grow back, you know."

"Thanks for the insight, little sister."

SaraJean looked at Kathy and me. "See what I mean?"

"How much one of those cost?" I asked.

"A lot," she said. "Although the VA would help some."

"Think you can swing it?"

"I'm workin' on it. Man, if it got him outta' here even one day a week, whatever it cost would be worth it."

"You'd think she doesn't like me around."

"Oh, Arlo. You know what I'm talking about. I love you, but you do get on my nerves."

"Hey. Who's the fucking invalid here? You or me?"

SaraJean's voice rose, in tenor and volume. "You are not a fucking invalid, Arlo. You are a healthy person who happens to be missing some pieces. I ain't sayin' I think it's fun for you, but for God's sake get off that damn pity pot and do something for yourself."

She stomped back out onto the porch.

Silence followed, except for Dick Van Dyke's laughter in the background.

"I know she's right," he said after an interminable pause. "I'm kind of afraid of what it's like out there. I haven't consorted with civilians, with a few exceptions such as yourselves, in years. Shit, if I was to drive, I'd probably have to quit smokin' reefer 24/7. And just as they're about to make it so I could legally smoke North Carolina-grown instead of this here Coloradan smoke."

"Now, there's a hardship," I said.

He looked at me with hard eyes. "You gave up drink, didn't you?"

I nodded.

The hard look came back before dissolving into tears.

Twelve

Monday

I could tell from the small crowd gathered around a booth half-way toward the back of the bakery that Nate had preceded me. When I came alongside the others, he said, "Mon. Come join us. Gabrielle, let my man have a seat."

A young woman with deep bronze skin and jet black hair slid off the bench opposite my lawyer friend. She stood up and up some more, well over six feet of her in a snug-fitting sweater and a skirt she had to yank down so as to not be guilty of indecent exposure. She smiled at me and I fell in love.

"Look over this way, Counselor," Nate said, "before you have a heart attack."

My face was burning like it had in middle school when a girl I liked kissed me.

"Rick Ryder," the big man said, holding an arm toward me while looking at Gabrielle and two other young women, only less attractive than their taller companion by degree. "Principle in Peters and Ryder Investigations, along with his wife, Kathy Peters." I wasn't sure if this was simple information-giving or to head off any possible misunderstandings. He was, after all, intimately familiar with my history.

He turned toward me while with his hand he identified the women. "These young ladies, Gabrielle, Yolanda, and Desirée, are the heart of my team defending Arthur Redmayne. You may remember me telling you of the gentleman who was arrested after he vocally objected to the treatment his son received vis-à-vis that given to white boys involved in the same incident. Gabrielle and Yolanda are paralegals. Desirée is interning with me as part of her last year at Duke Law." He turned back to his young associates. "I'll catch up with y'all at the office."

I kept eyes on Nate as they walked off.

"How do you do it, Nate?"

"What is the 'it' of which you speak?"

I shook my head. "Well, that was a nice start to the business day."

"In case you think the ladies are merely arm candy, I am actually hoping Desirée will take over my practice. You know, we've talked about the issues of 'driving while black' and even 'walking while black'. Well, attractive women of color have always had an extra burden. Along with the usual harassment women get, especially good-looking women, is the assumption that if they're particularly good looking, they must be hookers—by the police and by men in general. So, my advice when I talk to women is to become proficient in something that has nothing to do with the fact you are a woman. And embrace your womanhood, your beauty, and your proficiency equally. Now, Gabrielle is, admittedly, special. But you know who I like seeing just as much. A woman named Bountiful—really, her given name—who truly is. Woman must weigh two-fifty. Big woman. Big woman. She sings in the church choir. Solos. When she stands up, you'd think she'd had basic training at Quantico. You know what I'm sayin'? Proud. Big and black and proud. And that voice. You know opera?"

"A little."

"You know Leontyne Price?"

"I do."

"A voice like that. That's what I encourage young women to do. Get good at something. Be proud of it. Be like a Marine. One of the few, one of the proud."

"Counselor. You are on a roll this morning."

He slumped back in the booth. "Truth is, I'm runnin' out of juice, Rick. I think that's why I got on my soap box, there. It's time for others to take over. I couldn't be happier than if it was a woman. And if Desirée did that and the other two worked with her, she'd go to the top. She'd be in elected office in a few years. You know who she reminds me of? Michelle Obama. Smart, sassy, good-lookin'. I want to ask you, who, besides a dyed-in-the-wool racist does not like Michelle? Oh, shit. I'm off on another one. Whatta you have this morning?"

I burst out laughing. "Mr. Chatham," I said, "I am so grateful to have your acquaintance. My life would be so much poorer, colorless even, without you."

I got a semi-load of black smile in return. It didn't do to me what Gabrielle's did, but it was almost as satisfying.

"So, Counselor, how's the Revis case going?"

"First things first, Nate. We saw Queenie yesterday. She doesn't look good. More tired than even you appear. The woman's never tired. As her neighbor pointed out, she's only seventy-four, hardly qualifies as an old woman these days, and especially not her."

"That's the first I've heard. Haven't spoken to her recently. Might have to give her a call."

"I think that would be good. You know that if she's having any kind of medical problem it's going to take a court order and a helicopter in there to get her to see a doctor."

He smiled again, nodded. "Yeah. She can be kinda hard-headed."

"Kinda? Anyway, I want to run our list of suspects by you. Get your take. Starting with the aforementioned Ms. Weaver."

I thought he was going to spit his coffee across the table. Instead, he merely coughed. "Queenie? You jest."

"I know it seems unlikely. But she does have a motive. She knew the man and his habits. She certainly had the opportunity."

"If that woman put up with bein' called a nigger-lover back in the day because she hung out with me, got spit on, all that stuff, without killin' anyone, she wouldn't kill your Professor Revis. Oh, if he lived, and people started buying up land around her, she'd raise sand, that's for sure. But that's what she does. Raises sand. She's not gonna kill anybody."

"That's good historical perspective. And it's hard to think of her as a murderer. Although there's still the accidental overdose scenario. She goes down to the cabin with him, wants to make sure everything's all right for her guest. She finds the sleeping pills in the bathroom, doses up another drink for him. He passes out. She looks for the money and either finds it or doesn't. She leaves. The professor comes to, staggers around out into the barn. The next day when he doesn't show up at her house, she goes down there expecting to find him hungover, maybe still asleep. Instead finds him dead. She knows she has to call the law. Cleans her fingerprints off the glass he's been drinking out of and the sleeping pill bottle. Other than that, she doesn't worry, since her prints would ordinarily be all over the place. It is her cabin."

"Been doin' some thinking about that."

"I have, Nate. That's our job, you know?"

"Okay. That's one. Who else is on your list?"

"The Calhouns."

"The Calhouns? How are they involved in this?"

I told him the story.

"They're some interesting characters, that's for sure. And that's a lot of money you're talkin' about. But I don't see them getting messed up in murder, either. I do believe there've been more than a few broken bones and mashed-in faces that can be attributed to them, but, so far at least, murder doesn't seem to be part of their M.O. What they're more likely to do is twist—and I mean in the literal sense—twist the arms of people they heard might be looking at land on which to compete with them. And, as you found out, they do have an inclination toward harassment. Those Boggs boys are more or less at their service I understand. My guess is that if you hadn't intervened with them, they would have kept upping the ante out at your place until even someone as thick-headed as you would get the message."

"Counselor, you can bad mouth me anytime you want but I will not have you disparaging my wife. She lives out there, too, you know?"

Nate smiled again, a full one this time. I thought he'd make a great Santa Claus.

"I do have to say I liked the way you pulled off settin' them up like you did. That was pretty clever. Okay. So, anyone else on your list?"

I ran the Anne and Art scenario by him.

"I like the Shakespearean nature of it. Mother and son do in the old man. Make a good play. What else?"

"Here's another team effort," I said, and told him about the Philips-Ballard cabal.

"I like it," he said.

"What is it you like about it?"

"Lust. Intrigue. Betrayal. Murder. It might be better than the son and ex-wife plot."

"This is not a play, Nate."

He held up a big, black hand, the size of a catcher's mitt. "I know. This is serious stuff we got here. Man killed. Hundreds of thousands of dollars gone missing. Terrible thing. Well, my man, look around. There are terrible things going on all over, right here in River City. But, if we can't have a little fun in spite of it all, we might as well hang up the cleats."

***

When I returned to our second floor office, Kathy was deep into her role as Business Manager for Peters and Ryder Private Detective Agency.

"I'm glad you're here. I'm having a hard time figuring out what to charge Queenie. We've done a lot of work on this—cost is no object, I believe she said—but we did a lot of travel together that the case didn't really require."

"You're trying to be fair."

"Of course I'm trying to be fair," she snapped. The subtext, as I heard it, was Don't be such a jerk.

"Charge everything," I said, "all our trips together, everything, then cut it in half. Our 'Preferred Customer' discount. I think that'll wind up fair and I don't think the IRS can argue with it. That way you don't have to worry about the specifics of this or that trip and whether we were both 'needed.'"

"We haven't done that before when we've been working for Nate."

"Well, one, I don't thing we made any trips together that didn't require us both. And, two, we hadn't established the 'Preferred Customer' discount at that time."

"You know, sometimes I'm resentful that I have to do the books. At others, like this, I'm glad you aren't one of those 'in-charge' guys who think they ought to take care of everything."

"That is what I believe is called a left-handed compliment. The second of those I've gotten recently. I think Audrey needs some exercise. Maybe I'll encounter an epiphany while I'm in the woods."

Upon hearing 'woods,' the dog was up on all fours, tail working like it does when food is presented, looking intently at me, his unspoken message being, "Okay! Come on! You said, 'woods.' Let's go! Woods."

Rather than take the road, we trudged up the hill behind the house. The previous owners of the place had situated a split-log bench in a spot from where I could sit and ponder the eternal verities and Audrey could entertain the fantasy that he was going to catch some other species of wildlife. I made the mistake of throwing a stick, setting off a game which would have no end if he had his way. He eventually found something more interesting to chase, leaving me alone with my thoughts.

I began putting together the Colorado connections. The Professor, of course, and Cheri Ballard. Colorado. "Rocky Mountain High," the old John Denver song came to mind. Which led, inexorably, to Arlo and his Colorado bud? I wondered who his source was since he didn't go anywhere. SaraJean? Some "delivery person"? If SaraJean was Arlo's supplier, who was hers? Queenie? Who would have gotten it from Revis. That would be easy enough to check.

Audrey came back with a new stick and dropped it at my feet. I tried to ignore him. He picked it up again and dropped it again. Surrendering my quest for quiet contemplation, I played toss and return with him all the way down the hill to the house. He was disappointed I wouldn't let him bring his new toy inside.

I briefly related my musings to Kathy before calling Queenie.

"This may seem like a strange question," I began. "Did you

get any pot from the professor?"

"From the Pot Professor? Yeah. And, you know, I think maybe that's what's been wrong with me. Don't get me wrong. It was some righteous weed. Real fine. Maybe too fine for an occasional indulger. I think I might have been in withdrawal from it. Depressed, you know. I'm feelin' better now. Anyway, why are you askin'?"

"Did you give any to SaraJean?"

"Nope."

"Not even some to take back to Arlo?"

"You deaf this mornin', Ryder. No. I didn't give her any. I've never been in the distribution game and not gonna start now. Come on, out with it. What's up?"

I was reluctant to share my thoughts, but knew I wouldn't get off the phone until I did. "Arlo's been talking about this Colorado bud he's been smoking."

"Hmm."

"Yes. My thoughts, exactly. Hmm. So, I was wondering if maybe SaraJean visited the professor at the cabin."

"I don't like where this is goin', Rick."

"Me neither."

***

We have a whiteboard in our office, like the ones they use in TV or movie portrayals of detectives at work—usually accompanied by acting and action: lots of discussion and moving information and sticky notes around. In the real life of this detective, the only action involved sitting and staring at my desk, and not getting any closer to understanding who killed Professor Revis. I was relieved when the phone rang.

"Ryder, you ole whore. What're you up to?"

"Hey, Arlo. Oh, solving crimes, keepin' the residents of Buncombe County safe. You know, same ol', same ol'."

"Well, why don't you let the good citizens of the county fend for themselves a bit and come on out. Got something to show you."

"Going to give me any clues?"

"Nope. Just come on out. There'll even be some fresh coffee when you get here."

"There's an offer I can't refuse. Kathy's out checking on a wayward lover so I've got all the time in the world."

"That's okay. You just get your ass out here."

The man sounded positively sunny. I wondered if he'd put a little cocaine into the mix of intoxicants he was taking— although he wasn't exhibiting the manic quality coke users tend to radiate. He seemed happy. Engaging, even.

The sky was now a sea of gray mottled with black waves, enough to raise hopes that it could mean rain, a commodity in unusually scarce supply the last several months.

I gave the CD changer a voice command. Dire Straits came on singing about the "Sultans of Swing," a fine, feel-good song. By now the car could practically drive itself to the southwest side of Weaver Mountain. The reason for Arlo's call was apparent as I approached the bridge. The old gray van was nowhere in sight. In its place was a newer, shinier, longer version. It took up most of the gravel drive. Arlo was on the front porch.

"What have we here?" I asked as I approached.

"Oh, man. This is the coolest," Arlo said, motoring his chair down from the porch to meet me. "You've got to see this." He motioned to a ramp protruding from the back end of the van like the tongue of some prehistoric lizard. "Go on inside. I can drive this thing up in there. Clamps automatically grab onto my chair. Tie downs."

The only seat was shotgun, leaving clear sailing for Arlo.

"I imagine you know all about voice commands and steering wheel instruments," he said. "Look at all that stuff. I can do everything from there, man. Who needed those damn legs, anyway? Just something extra to take care of, clippin' toenails and all that."

I was impressed. "Arlo, you are positively ecstatic about this. I think it means you'll be getting out of the house."

"Yeah, man. And I'm scared to death."

"About driving this thing?"

"Well, that. It's a huge mother. But I drove bigger in Nam. And I won't be taking incoming while I'm at the wheel. It's more about other people. You know, how they react. Oh, look at that poor man. That kind of crap. That's really what's kept me in the house. Well, that and the pot. Can't say the bud of the Cannabis sativa plant has ever made me want to get up and do something. But then the pot's really been a way to cope with being stuck in the house. Well, that and not having any legs. That's kind of a bummer."

"I imagine."

"Yeah ... So, when SaraJean pulled into the drive with this yesterday afternoon, at first I was like, oh, shit, now what. But maybe it's all the bells and whistles. It's crazy. I'm excited about driving it. There are a couple of problems, though and you might be able to help me out with one of them."

"Oh?"

"I don't have a driver's license. Well, I have one but it expired while I was over getting' my legs shot off. I thought maybe you could go with me to get a new one. Probably have to get a learner's permit."

"Arlo, man. I'd be honored. But I would have thought that

SaraJean ... "

"Bless her heart," he interrupted. "I love her. You know I do. But I'm gonna be nervous enough as it is and I'd be skittish as a cat with her sittin' next to me, tryin' to be helpful."

"You'll have to practice somewhere. This isn't like driving some Chevy with all the standard equipment—which I imagine is kinda what you last drove."

"1970, 426 V8 Barracuda, 727 automatic transmission, slapstick shifter." He sighed, not unlike after orgasm. "Now there was a car. Don't make 'em like that anymore, do they."

"Nah. Something about fuel economy, the environment, stuff like that. And where is your sister, anyway?"

"Up to Queenie's. Some people are comin' to look at her goats, maybe buy 'em. Queenie's afraid she might fall to pieces if she has to watch 'em go."

"Oh, man. That'll be hard on her, I know."

We agreed that I'd come over the next day. I hoped I'd get to see SaraJean so I could tell her how impressed I was with Arlo's transformation. He was like a kid with a new toy and he hadn't even gotten to use it. On the way home I thought about how much it might have cost. $50,000? $100,000? I had no idea. I also realized I hadn't asked about the provenance of the marijuana he'd been smoking. Maybe because he hadn't smoked anything while I'd been there.

Back at my desk I stared up at the whiteboard in the hope that it would spontaneously highlight the name or names of those responsible for Marc Revis's death. The ringing of the phone again distracted me from all I wasn't doing.

"Who the hell do you think you are, Ryder, coming down here, insinuating that I was responsible for the death of Marc

Revis? If you don't quit harassing me and the people I work with, I'm going to sue you for slander and defamation of character."

"Hello, Professor Philips," I said, using my formal, hard-edged but polite tough-guy voice. "Apparently you missed the part about me being an investigator. That's my job. I ask questions. It's unfortunate if asking questions about your connections to Professor Revis may seem to imply that you were involved in his demise."

"Cut the shit, Ryder. I'm serious about this. Leave me and the people I work with alone."

I love it when I get ultimatums. "You need to know, Dr. Philips, that I will continue to pursue this case as long as necessary and will follow it wherever it leads. You also might be interested in knowing that I am a lawyer myself and am familiar with slander and defamation law, so if you decide to sue me you'd do well to get the assistance of very good counsel. Unless you have anything else to add, good day, Professor Philips." I cut off the call before he had a chance to tell me whether or not he had anything to add.

Kathy was standing in the doorway. "What was that about?"

"Philips wants me to back off. Gonna sue me if I don't."

"And when was it that you learned about slander and defamation law?"

"I practiced environmental law, if you'll remember. Whenever we filed complaints against polluters they threatened us with lawsuits for exactly those reasons. They never stood up as long as we had credible evidence that what we were accusing them of was true."

"Do we have that kind of evidence against Philips?"

"I think there's enough evidence to justify asking the questions we've asked of the people we've asked them."

"Does the phone call increase or decrease your sense of his involvement in Revis's death?"

"Good question. I'm actually inclined to think it decreases it. It sounded like he's more pissed off about what this will do to his reputation than him being implicated in the murder."

"Couldn't that be ego? The idea that his reputation might suffer is more threatening to him than whether or not he gets arrested?"

"Sure, it could be. And, once again, I understand the sheriff's decision not to pursue this case in the absence of any physical evidence that would challenge the idea of a self-inflicted occurrence. Absent the 'smoking gun,' I'm not sure where to go next."

"What happened to that? You were all excited after you got that picture from Art. You seemed to think you were on to something."

"I think I got a little ahead of myself." I paused, then added, "But somehow I do believe it points the right way. It's like when you're near someone who points out something in the distance and you can't make out exactly what it is they want you to see. That's how this is."

"It's out there somewhere," she said.

"Yeah."

She nodded and shrugged simultaneously. I took it for uncertainty, perhaps a lack of confidence that what I was saying made any sense.

"On another note entirely, while you were out sleuthing, Arlo called." I proceeded to fill her in on our friend's new vehicle. "It's very neat. He can drive his wheelchair right up the back of it into the driver's spot where it automatically locks the chair down. All the controls are either hand- or voice-operated. He's like a kid with a new toy—and he wants me to go to the

DMV with him to get his learner's permit."

"Wow. Talk about an attitude adjustment."

"I think a part of him not getting out of the house has been because he'd have to go with SaraJean wherever he went, which just reinforces his dependency on her."

"And his resentment."

"Exactly. So, I'll be out there about nine tomorrow and we'll get him on the road to transportational independence."

"Sounds epic."

"Could be."

Thirteen

Tuesday

As I expected, Arlo was out on the front porch—and he was just like a kid waiting for the bus on the first day of school. I was surprised to find him wearing a camo shirt, presumably a relic from his time in service.

"What's with the garb?" I asked. "Never thought I'd see you grace those threads again."

"Figure it can't hurt with those bureaucrats out there."

SaraJean was grinning when she came out to join us. "I can't tell you how grateful I am that you're doing this, Rick. I understand why he wanted someone other than me. I really do. And you're about the only other person he's had much to do with for a while."

"I'm glad to be able to do it. I was fortunate that I didn't have to go to war as a young man and this seems to be a small way to—"

"Can we can the nobility crap and get going?"

The new ramp from the porch made for an easy transition to the van. SaraJean said he'd been out there since 7:00 working all the controls he could while the van was stationary.

With three arms and two legs between us, it was a minor challenge to move the seat that was in the passenger's spot over to the driver's side. Arlo then maneuvered into the empty space.

Once he got his learner's permit, we'd switch places.

As he was driving up the ramp, he said, "I think I might throw up." Handing me a Lynyrd Skynyrd CD, the old southern-rock band. "Once we get out of the drive, crank that sucker up," he commanded.

The controls for someone with no legs to work the pedals are different than those for a guy with only one arm. I managed to get the hang of them with only a couple of hair-raising mishaps.

"Jesus!" he yelled after I'd come close to rear-ending a 16-wheeler. "I don't mind a little irony in my life, but to lose it in a car wreck after surviving…"

"Yeah," I cut him off. "I get it."

The DMV process went without a hitch and we were back at the top of his drive at 10:30.

"You know what song you gotta replay for SaraJean?"

I hesitated for a moment before choosing the last cut on the album, the band's classic, Freebird.

SaraJean was waiting at the bottom of the ramp when we descended. She and her brother began laughing, we all slapped hands. There were hugs all around during which she began to cry.

"I'm sorry. It's just so … incredible. I was really afraid you'd never get out of the house again."

"It's okay, little sis," Arlo said before his voice began to crack.

When they'd regained composure, SaraJean asked, "Everything seem to be in good working order?"

"Vehicle wise, yeah, man," Arlo said. "It was great!" He gave a sly glance toward me. "Not sure about all the operators, though."

"Yeah, well," I said, "the only thing I noticed was that

the shotgun seat was a little shaky after we moved the seats around. I think it probably just needs to have a couple of bolts tightened."

SaraJean started for the shed.

"That's okay," I said. "I can get it now that I'm part of this project."

"Won't have any trouble finding one," Arlo said. "She's got that place as shipshape as a, well, as a ship."

"Wrenches are on the left hand wall when you walk in," she said.

Arlo was right about the place being shipshape. A place for everything and everything in its place. I thought about Queenie's "little" barn and figured SaraJean had been responsible for organizing that, too. I grabbed a couple of wrenches from a neat arrangement where she said they'd be. When I turned to leave, something caught my eye that didn't seem to belong. A smallish automobile tire was leaned up against the opposite wall. If I hadn't gotten the photos from Art Revis I may not have thought anything about it.

"Wow," I said to SaraJean when I was outside. "You sure know how to organize a space. I need to get you out at our place. The basement is a disaster."

A smile stretched her cheeks. "Any time. I understand you're quite the one-armed cook. Fix me a meal and I'll take care of it."

Tightening the seat was a simple task even for me. After returning the tools I took a closer look at the tire. I glanced outside to be sure I wasn't being watched, then bent down to read the size. My gut did a flip. I felt like a prospector in the old West, coming across a vein of gold, not knowing how to use the knowledge without giving away his secret.

SaraJean asked if I'd like something to drink but I was afraid they'd catch on that something was up with me if I stayed.

"Thanks, but no. I need to get back to the detective business. I do appreciate the opportunity to get the slug here back out into the world."

After another round of hugs, I was on my way, hoping I hadn't appeared overly anxious to leave.

I bounded up the stairs to our office two at a time.

"You break the case?" Kathy asked when I appeared at the doorway, breathless.

"Not quite. But we may be getting close. I'll explain in a minute."

On a Jaguar website, I typed in tire sizes for the XJS and scrolled to 1991. Of the two it showed, one was 235/60R15—exactly what I'd seen at the Pressley's. I pumped my fist in the air as if I'd hit a three-point shot.

Her eyes were wide with expectation. "What?"

After I explained, she asked, "Is that enough to take to the police?"

"I'm not sure this changes anything for them. And, we don't actually know that we've found the smoking gun. Only the holster."

"What about telling Queenie?"

"I want to talk to Nate first."

With some slick talking, I got Natasha to interrupt her boss long enough to schedule a meeting for that afternoon.

After what would have been, under other circumstances, a pleasant leisurely lunch at a favorite downtown hangout, Kathy and I walked to Nate's office.

"Natasha tells me you've busted this thing," he said when we were all seated in his conference room.

"Not altogether, but I think we know where the money is. Or was."

"Pray tell."

"The other day I was moving papers around on my desk and came across pictures I'd printed of the '91 Jaguar XJS, the kind Revis drove, and saw something that got me curious. Unlike most cars that have the spare in a well in the trunk, in this particular model the spare stands against the firewall in back of the passenger compartment. I didn't remember seeing a tire there when Art Revis showed the car off to me. So I got him to take a picture of the inside of the trunk and send it to me. I was right. There was an empty space where the tire should have been. Would someone really drive fifteen-hundred miles without a spare? Later, when Kathy and I were talking about where you might stash that much cash, the idea of it being in the tire flashed in my mind. I did some calculations with the help of the internet and found that a million dollars really wouldn't take up a lot of space."

"How much is 'not a lot.'"

I explained what I'd learned, that a stack of a hundred hundred-dollar bills is about .43 inches high—a little more if the bills are used and crinkly. And the standard tire for that car has an outside diameter of 26.9" and a width of 8.5".

"So a million bucks would be forty-three inches high. The interior circumference would be about eighty-one inches. You'd have way more space than you needed."

Nate leaned his huge frame back in his chair and nodded. "You take the tire off the rim and stash the money inside, wrapped in small packages to keep it from flying all around and getting' tore up, put the tire back on in working condition."

"Right where it's supposed to be," I said.

"And you have found the felonious tire?"

"I have. When I was out with Arlo getting his learners permit to drive this fancy new van SaraJean bought him, I saw a tire—what I took be the tire—in their shed. Turns out that SaraJean is a bit compulsive, everything in its right place. Except for this tire, leaning lonely against a wall. Very out of place."

"All right, Counselor," he said. "Speaking for the defense, you have a tire out there which matches the description of a tire that would fit the professor's Jag. How do you know that is the tire from the automobile in question?"

"It would explain where the cash came from to buy Arlo's new and very expensive van. And the only vehicles we've seen out there are SaraJean's truck, their old van, and this new van. None of them would have that kind of tire. The Jaguar is missing a spare tire. And, to repeat, the size of the tire I saw is the size of a tire that would fit the Jaguar."

"So," the lawyer said, "the tire at her place is the one that had been in the professor's automobile and is now missing from said automobile. None of that puts SaraJean in the cabin the night Professor Revis died. In fact, I don't believe there is any evidence that Ms. Pressley committed a crime. As far as we know, the authorities have no idea that tire ever existed. My guess is that the people who supplied the money in question aren't going to come forward."

"You don't think we need to take this information to the sheriff?" I asked.

"I think your friend Detective Fair would likely say, 'What money?' So far as we know, no one's called up and said, 'Hey, there's a million dollars floatin' around down there and, oh, yeah, it's money no one wants to claim.' Unless I have misunderstood about SaraJean, I imagine that if she came upon that tire and that money, the money now will be nowhere to be found. I'd guess it's in the ground somewhere. From Fair's point of view, without the money what's the motive for killing the man? And there is still no evidence that he was killed and that it wasn't a case of an overdose, either intentional or suicidal. I believe they are perfectly happy to let the thing lie. They might even get annoyed with you for muddying the waters."

"He wouldn't care that SaraJean might have hastened Professor Revis's demise so she could get the money?"

"What money?" the big man repeated.

"Damn it," I barked. "I still want to know—our client wants to know—what really happened out there."

"Gee, Rick," Nate said. "You may have to go ask SaraJean what she knows. Isn't that what investigators do? Interrogate the suspects?"

"If—and this is a big 'if'—SaraJean was responsible for the professor's death, I'd still like to know about the Calhouns. What were they up to with the Boggs boys?"

"Let's have that chat after you find out if you've really found the smoking gun."

***

On the way home, Kathy asked, "How do you see this thing going down if SaraJean is, in fact, the perpetrator?"

"I think Nate's right. We have to ask her how it is she came upon the tire. There's also the issue of the Colorado dope Arlo's been smoking and is blithely ignorant of any need to keep that quiet. Where did that come from?"

"And the Philips-Ballard conspiracy?" she asked.

"Still on the table, I guess. But the tire in SaraJean's garage is pretty damning in my mind. We need to have a 'Come to Jesus' with that girl."

"Girl?" Kathy asked. "Did you really say 'girl'?"

"I did and I take it back. That woman."

"Do you think Queenie needs to be there?"

Fourteen

Wednesday

A front came through overnight, bringing with it that particular shade of blue sky in which Carolinians believe they have a proprietary interest. It also delivered a noticeable drop in the temperature. If we hadn't been distracted by what we were about to confront, we might have thought to take jackets or sweaters. We weren't paying attention. We were nervous. They were friends of ours. What, I wondered, if SaraJean denied involvement? What if Queenie went to her defense?

Like a river pilot guiding a ship into harbor, Sonny guided us the last fifty yards to the house. The two women were seated on the porch.

"Little chilly out here," Queenie said. "I've got a couple of sweatshirts if you want. Or we can go to go inside. Seems a little too nice to waste this weather, though."

We nodded, and she led Kathy inside to find sweatshirts that would fit us.

"Arlo still excited about the van?" I asked SaraJean before she could speak.

"He is. He even talked to the VA about how he might get involved out there. It's made a huge difference, Rick. You can't believe. I thought that he'd like the idea of being able to get around without me, but I couldn't have hoped for this kind of transformation."

When the other two women ~~reappeared~~ rejoined us and we'd pulled the rocking chairs close so we could have a conversation, Queenie asked, "Okay. So, what's going on you needed to talk to us? You got this crime solved?"

"We think we're close." Turning my attention to the younger woman, I said, "And we believe you might be able to help us fill in some pieces."

SaraJean's posture stiffened; her eyes seemed to grow. "How can I help?"

"Well," I began, stalling. "When I was out at your place, after going with Arlo to the DMV, you'll recall that I went into your shed. When I was in there, I saw a car tire leaning up against the wall."

A mask dropped over her face.

"It's the same size as a tire that that would fit the late Marc Revis's Jaguar."

"Anyone want to fill me in on what this is about?" Queenie asked.

"Hold on, Queenie," Kathy said. "We're getting there."

"You could help, SaraJean, by telling us where you were the night Dr. Revis died."

"Where I was?"

"Yes, SaraJean. Where you were."

She looked over to Queenie as if to say, Help! "Well. I was up here for a while and then I went home."

In unison, Kathy and I looked at the older woman.

She shrugged. "That's what I remember."

"Okay," I said, "time to cut the shit, if you'll excuse my language." Leaning into our suspect, I said, "Why don't you tell us how that tire, a tire you would have no use for, wound up in your garden shed."

After another few seconds of stony silence, I asked, "Do I need to help you out here?"

"I still need help here," Queenie said. "I'm really in the dark."

I turned to her.

"There is a car tire in the Pressleys' shed completely out of place with everything else. We believe it's the spare tire from Dr. Revis's car." I turned back to SaraJean. "Is that right?"

She remained unmoved, as if she'd become catatonic.

"And we believe it's where the money Dr. Revis carried from Colorado was stashed."

At last, she broke. Her eyes closed, her head drooped.

"The good part of it is we think that's where SaraJean got the money to buy Arlo's new van."

Queenie, now bug-eyed, turned to her neighbor. "Is this true, honey?"

SaraJean's slow nod was almost imperceptible. No one said anything. The wind carried the leading edge of fall past us.

"We still don't know what happened up at the cabin before you took the tire."

Tears began to form and slide slowly down SaraJean's cheeks.

"I didn't kill him. I didn't even know he was dead until I heard about it the next morning. I thought he'd just passed out." She looked over at Queenie as if for permission to continue but now the older woman's demeanor turned stony.

"I'd been up here with Queenie when Dr. Revis came by that evening ... "

I shot Queenie a glance. She'd not told us about that. As if reading my mind, she said, "I didn't think it mattered."

I let my glare linger before turning back to SaraJean. "Go on."

"Anyway, we all drank bourbon and smoked some pot, some of his pot. Boy, that stuff was strong. He was all full of himself. I didn't really like the guy. He started going on about how he was going to bring legal pot to North Carolina, as if he single-handedly was going to make it happen. He told us about the money and how nobody would find it, like he was brilliant. I don't know what happened then. I just got the idea that I could find the money."

The tears turned into sobs.

The rest of us leaned forward involuntarily.

When her sobbing subsided enough that she could make herself understood, she said, "I worry so much about Arlo. I'm scared to death of what will happen to him if I'm not around. When I heard about the money, I thought about buying a van he could drive without my help and I could put enough away to help take of him if something happened to me."

Kathy asked, "Is something wrong, SaraJean? Something you've not been talking about?"

"No." Her voice rose in pitch. She sounded like a little girl. "But, you know, stuff happens. I mean an accident, or I could get sick. That's why I've been keeping myself in shape, to stay healthy. But, shit just happens, you know? And he can't take care of himself. I mean, he does pretty good, considering all the pot he smokes, and I don't blame him for that."

"Arlo know you feel like this?" Queenie asked.

"No. And don't you go tellin' him, neither."

More silence, like a pall, hung over us.

"Well," I said. "So, you went down to the cabin ... "

"Right after Dr. Revis left here I said to Queenie I ought to be going. When I knocked on the door down there, you shoulda seen the man's face. This lecherous look, like I'd come down there for, you know ... "

"Sex," Kathy offered.

SaraJean grinned. "Yeah. With that old man? God, he's like, what, seventy or something."

"Hey," Queenie objected. "Careful what you're sayin' about seventy-year olds."

"Sorry. But you know what I'm saying. So of course he invites me in, asks me if I want a drink. I mean he was kinda wobbly already. I said, sure, I'd have another. Then I said, and I know this was probably wrong, but I said, 'I thought you were an alcoholic or something.' He just smiled and said, 'Special occasion.' Oh, really, I thought. So, he pours us a glass each, puts ice and a little water in mine, like I had it up here with you, Queenie. Then he lights a joint. I said I'd pass on that. I mean, I was just on the edge of being wasted myself. I was trying to get him to talk about the money, you know, say where it was. I didn't know what I'd do next, figured I'd go home for a while till he got sleepin' good, then come back to look for it. Really. I mean, I wasn't plannin' on stealin' a million dollars. I can't hardly believe it." She paused and said, "I could use some more coffee. Anyone else?"

We all passed. While she was in the house getting a refill, the three of looked at each other, no one saying a word, pondering the moment.

When she returned, she picked up her narrative as though she hadn't been gone. "Then he went to the bathroom. When he came back he had this pill bottle, said they were sleeping pills and did I want any. I said I didn't think it was good to take sleeping pills with alcohol. He said something like, 'Shit, I haven't been able to sleep right for twenty years, this is the only stuff that works,' and then, and I can't hardly believe my eyes, he dumps a bunch into his hand and throws them in his mouth. I don't know, maybe it was because he was drunk and not thinkin' straight, but it seemed to me like a pretty dumb thing to do to. Anyway, then I said something like, 'So you've hidden that money pretty good, huh?' He said, 'It's in the spare tire.' Just like that, like it was no big deal. 'The spare tire?' I asked. He said, 'Yeah, come on and I'll show you,' and we headed out the back door. He was real unsteady now, but we went into the little barn and he reached for the light and he fell. I thought he'd tripped or something. He'd thrown his arms out like he was going to catch somethin', but there wasn't nothin' there to catch. It didn't seem like he'd hit anything, but he was out like a light. Just passed out I guessed. I looked around and saw the tire. And I think to myself, you can't do this.' And then I think, why the he ... heck not? I mean, what's this money going to do? Buy land to grow pot on. Not like some big thing, you know, good for society like cure cancer or anything."

We let that settle in.

"And the rest," I offered, "is, as they say, history. And you didn't go to the police when you heard he had died because ... "

"They might not believe me and they'd want the money back. Are you going to have to tell them what happened?"

"What happened? You mean that they've been right all along. The man died of an accidental overdose."

"What about the money?" SarahJean asked.

"What money?" I looked to Kathy. "We've not seen any money, have we?"

"Not me."

"I would, however," I added, "get rid of that tire if I were you."

On the way home, Kathy asked, "What are you going to tell Detective Fair?"

"That from what we can tell, it's as they've said all along. Accidental, self-inflicted. As far as we know, no one has reported any money missing. There's Philip's crazy idea that the man had brought a million dollars with him. Other than that, unless the people who provided the money come forward, it seems like that was just a figment of someone's imagination."

"What if the money people themselves come looking for it. It wouldn't be hard for them to find out where Revis had stayed."

"You think they'll shake down Queenie to find out where it is?" I asked.

"They might."

"Good luck with that."

***

When I told Detective Fair that our investigation had confirmed the sheriff's department's findings, he said he appreciated our work and that the county could rest easier now. I told him not to be a dork. There was no mention of money.

I told Art Revis and Anne McDonald the same thing: our investigation had confirmed the sheriff's determination of self-administered ingestion of an overdose of sleeping pills and alcohol.

Kathy asked if I was going to talk to Dr. Philips. I felt no compunction about leaving him hanging although I would have liked it if someone wanted to fund a further investigation into the Philips-Ballard connection.

***

E xplain again what you think the Boggs boys were up to out at our place," Kathy said to Nate while we were sitting in his conference room.

"The way I hear it—"

"Hear from whom?" Kathy asked.

Nate looked out over the tops of his glasses, a look of mild disdain.

"When one's work of four, five decades routinely brings you in contact with the more colorful class of people in the community along with their handlers, one develops certain communication lines not open to the general public. One hears things that aren't published in the local paper. One is privy to—"

"Okay," Kathy said, "I get it. You have your sources."

"In a nutshell. So, my understanding, based upon extensive research and a finely tuned ear, is that, as I believe I may have mentioned, the Calhouns, who also have big ears, although theirs are attuned to a particular wave length, hear about a large sum of money headed this way for the express purpose of buying land on which marijuana will be grown. These people are not what you would call free-market adherents. Their business model does not include a lot of competition.

"When they hear that you two are involved, they assume that your task is to find the money, not what really happened to Dr. Revis. They don't give a hoot what happened to him and can't imagine anyone else would either. Of course, as it turned out you were, indeed, looking for the money, although in the service of a higher goal."

Kathy made an ostentatious glance at her watch.

"You're the one who asked the question," Nate said. "Don't worry, I'm getting' there. So, they don't want more competition. One way to deal with it is to take the money Revis had out of circulation. If you find it, they're afraid you'll return it to its rightful owners, who will then find someone else to front their land purchases."

"They want us to stop looking for the money," I said.

"That's how I hear it."

"Why aren't they looking for the money instead of harassing us? If we hadn't found the money it wouldn't mean no one else would."

"They assumed that if someone else found the money, someone with less noble interests than you two have, that person or persons would use it for themselves. Precisely what happened with the Pressleys."

"So, they send these bozos to scare us off the hunt," Kathy said.

"I know you think these guys are incompetent. And I'm not suggesting that the decks they play with are completely full. However, they did get your attention. I believe that if you'd not been there on their last outing, they would have made it more clear what they were up to, what it was that they expected from you. And along the way, they are letting you know that they can get to you. Even with a nosy neighbor. If fact, they might have started going after him as well."

"I don't know," Kathy said. "It seems like a real one-off. And these guys are major players in the pot game?"

"I don't believe anybody ever said that growin' pot made you smart."

***

As soon as I got back to Cove Road, I joined Kathy on the deck.

"Do you believe SaraJean's story?" she asked.

"It's credible enough. That's all a good story has to be. You know how I feel about marijuana, how stupid I think our way of trying to control the use of it is. And I believe that the ends to which the million dollars Professor Marcus Revis brought to town went to a much better cause than that for which it had been intended."

"What about what Arlo said about seeing a gray van? Seemed like we were seeing them everywhere."

"I don't think he was out on the bridge that night. I imagine he was inside, looking out the front window, stoned, watching the moon. When SaraJean drove her old van home, across the bridge, he perceived it as going on down the road. By the next morning his memory of the event was pretty screwed up. In his mind that's what happened. A gray van came down the road and went on by."

A rlo called a few days later. He'd been working on his driving with SaraJean but wanted me to accompany him when he went to get his permanent license.

SarahJean greeted me on the porch the next morning, looking like a kid who'd been caught lying about what happened to her homework. Before she could say anything, I held my hand up to her, palm side out.

"Case closed. How's the boy doing?"

"Like he was the day you took him to get his learner's permit. Ready to go to off to kindergarten."

Arlo blabbed the whole way to the DMV, covering his nervousness, knowing the driving test would be extrarigorous for him. "I think the idea of a no-legged guy with a high tech vehicle is gonna unnerve them."

"Like it does you?"

"Yeah," he admitted. "Like that."

When he rolled back into the DMV waiting room after the exam, he could have been mistaken for a teenager getting his first license. They took his picture and gave him the temporary paper to use until the permanent document arrived in the mail.

Back on the Pressleys' porch, we hugged until the tears ran again. SaraJean looked at me with same questioning gaze she'd had earlier and again I waved her off.

"Now that the wall's been broken for Arlo, you guys need to come on out to Cove Road," I offered. "Audrey will be thrilled to see you. The cats probably not so much. And there's a dicey narrow bridge you need to be careful of."

Queenie invited us up so we could settle accounts. I told her we'd be up the next day. By then, Peters and Ryder's Investigations, LLC, would be ready to get back to work. In the meantime we were lolling about, enjoying the feeling of having successfully completed an important and difficult task. Kathy's eyes were closed, her breathing shallow, like she'd fallen asleep.

I wasn't convinced that she was completely over the effects of the crash. I thought about my own life-changing accident, recognizing that I'd suffered psychological after-effects for years. Although Kathy had not lost a limb, in my haste to have her be okay, to not have to worry about her, I'd avoided the reality that it might take her a long time to recover as well.

The creek murmured down the mountain. Audrey lay at our feet. The cats dozed out at the edges of the deck, as blasé as ever as to the workings of the world around them.

And life was good.

కి‿ఎ

About the Author

RF Wilson resides with his wife, Beth, in Asheville, NC. His thirty-plus years of experience in the addiction field have had a significant influence on his fiction writing. He is the author of nearly two dozen short stories and two previous Rick Ryder mysteries, *Deadly Dancing* and *Killer Weed*. When not writing, he spends his time pursuing his interests in music, movies, cosmology, philosophy, and hiking the Blue Ridge Mountains.

Also available from Pisgah Press

Mombie: The Zombie Mom	Barry Burgess	$16.95
Letting Go: Poems 1983-2003	Donna Lisle Burton	$14.95
Way Past Time for Reflecting		$17.95
From Roots ... to Wings		$14.95
Gabriel's Songbook	Michael Amos Cody	$17.95

Musical Morphine: Transforming Pain One Note at a Time $17.95
Robin Russell Gaiser
Finalist, USA Book Awards—Health: Alternative Medicine, 2017
Open for Lunch $17.95

rhythms on a flaming drum	Michael Hopping	$16.95

I Like It Here! Adventures in the Wild & Wonderful World of Theatre   C. Robert Jones
$30.00
                            Lanky Tales   C. Robert Jones
Lanky Tales, Vol. I: The Bird Man & other stories $9.00
Lanky Tales, Vol. II: Billy Red Wing & other stories $9.00
Lanky Tales, Vol. III: A Good and Faithful Friend & other stories $9.00
The Mystery at Claggett Cove $9.00

Reed's Homophones: A Comprehensive Book of Sound-alike Words   A. D. Reed
$14.95

Swords in their Hands: George Washington and the Newburgh Conspiracy   Dave Richards
$24.95   Finalist, USA Book Award—History 2014

Trang Sen: A Novel of Vietnam   Sarah-Ann Smith $19.50

Invasive Procedures: Earthqukes, Calamities, & poems from the midst of life   Nan Socolow
$17.95

The Rick Ryder Mystery Series   RF Wilson
Deadly Dancing $15.95
Killer Weed $14.95
The Pot Professor $17.95

Pisgah Press, LLC
PO Box 9663, Asheville, NC 28815-0663
www.pisgahpress.com

CPSIA information can be obtained
at www.ICGtesting.com
Printed in the USA
FFHW012135011019
55328647-61078FF